G000164447

GUARDING
THE
MERMAID

EVE LANGLAIS

Chimera Secrets 2 - Romantic Horror

Copyright © 2018/19, Eve Langlais

Cover Dreams2Media © 2018

Produced in Canada

Published by Eve Langlais ~ www.EveLanglais.com

eBook ISBN: 978 1 77 384 068 0

Print ISBN: 978 1 77 384 069 7

ALL RIGHTS RESERVED

This is a work of fiction and the characters, events and dialogue found within the story are of the author's imagination and are not to be construed as real. Any resemblance to actual events or persons, either living or deceased, is completely coincidental.

No part of this book may be reproduced or shared in any form or by any means, electronic or mechanical, including but not limited to digital copying, file sharing, audio recording, email, photocopying, and printing without permission in writing from the author.

CHAPTER ONE

THE VOMIT HIT HER RIGHT IN THE CHEST, thankfully missing her face. Not for the first time, Becky wondered why the heck she'd thought nursing was her calling.

It seemed like a good idea at the time, coming out of high school with no idea what to do. Her aunt, who acted as her guardian after her parents died in a car crash, touted the benefits of it. "Just think of it, Becky-bee,"—a nickname she'd once hated but now missed since her aunt had passed— "a guaranteed job no matter where you go." Sounded ideal.

With nothing better to do, Becky completed all the training, which proved more difficult than expected. But she persevered, and her aunt turned out to be right. Being a nurse had its perks, such as medical and dental insurance and the ability to work pretty much anywhere—not that she tested that theory, remaining in Edmonton, about two hours from the small town she grew up in.

The less glamorous aspects of nursing included projectile puke. Blood and other bodily fluids stained her scrubs on a daily basis. She had to learn to become nose blind to the smells. Dealt with the long hours. Harder, though, was the misery and the daily litany from families ranting at her to do something about their loved one.

"Fix him. Now." Often accusing Becky of not doing enough because the loved ones suffered under some notion she held back a special pill that instantly fixed all booboos. She wished she had a magical cure.

I'd use it on myself. Those lying in the beds weren't the only ones with problems. Having medical knowledge only meant she understood better than most the gravity of her issues. She lived on borrowed time.

At moments like this one, as she mopped the majority of the vomit from her chest—trying not to heave herself—she wished she'd pursued another path. Something that made her happy. Given her days on Earth were getting shorter and shorter, in her off time, which wasn't as plentiful as she'd hoped for, she studied journalism.

She ignored the naysayers that claimed the art of

news was dying. The need for people to know the truth would never cease. But she couldn't deny that the opportunities to make a good living at it proved difficult to find.

Newspapers showed no interest in an inexperienced journalist. They would never take Becky seriously until she came up with the story of a lifetime. The investigative piece that would make her mark and put her name on everyone's lips. A legacy that might make people remember her.

A story she'd never find working in a hospital all day long.

Exiting the lounge for nurses—which sounded fancier than the small room deserved with its pockmarked lockers, two bathroom stalls, trough sink, and warped mirror that belonged in a carnival—she heard a commotion coming from the emergency room. Which wasn't all that unusual. Most of the action in hospitals usually centered around incoming patients. Especially in the wee hours before dawn.

She'd yet to discern why the witching hour between midnight and four caused the most traumas. Drinking and drugs were only part of it. It was as if the crazy gene, the one that sent people galloping through the ER neighing and clomping like a horse or had them standing on a chair extolling the end of the world, activated most heavily in the dark of night.

The cacophony of excited voices continued, interspersed with screeching, the high-pitched squealing almost animal-like.

What on earth? Had someone brought in a pig? She'd seen stranger sights. Frantic children bringing in hamsters. Once even a squirrel.

She headed toward the center of confusion and saw a man, his hair long and messy, the snarled knots in need of scissors more than a comb. His clothes, the parts visible at least, appeared ragged where he drooped in the grips of two policemen. He wore an aluminum hat with more of the aluminum wrapped around his arms, chest, and thighs. Oddly enough, that wasn't the weirdest part of his appearance. Between the hanks of greasy hair, the man's eyes glowed yellow.

Like jack-o'-lantern glowed. She wondered what drugs he'd taken to cause that to happen because the effect certainly wasn't natural.

The man collapsed to the floor the moment the cops released him, hugging his knees, sobbing.

Becky neared enough to hear the police officers explaining the situation to the triage nurse—Jenny, a no-nonsense matron in her fifties who took pride in her nickname Battle Axe. Get in her way and she was liable to chop you off at the knees and have you emptying bedpans for a month.

"...found him in the park, scrounging through the garbage cans."

"Is he under the influence of alcohol or drugs?" Jenny made notes on a clipboard while the hobo with the freaky eyes and aluminum armor continued to keen, a guttural noise that raised all the hairs on Becky's body. He sounded afraid. A common occurrence. All too many people didn't trust hospitals or doctors.

The cop with a granite face and a lip bisected by an old scar shrugged. "We didn't find any drugs on him. Nor any signs of needle marks on his arms. We got him to blow, too. The breathalyzer showed nothing."

His partner, a younger fellow with tanned skin and glossy dark hair, added, "He could be high. You should have seen him scarfing down some discarded sub he found. I don't think he was even chewing he swallowed stuff so fast."

Jenny continued to tick off boxes. "Name?"

"No idea. We didn't find a wallet or anything that might identify him, and he's yet to answer any questions."

"Unless you can understand cave-man grunt," muttered the partner.

"Violent?" Jenny asked.

"Nope. Other than making noise, he didn't resist at all. But he's not been cooperative either." The hobo still sat hunched on the floor, head bowed, moaning.

"Escort him into cubicle nine. You"—the stern gaze of the triage nurse zeroed in on Becky—"get him started on some fluids and take his vitals." Jenny handed her the clipboard. "And put him into something clean. God only knows what vermin he's got crawling under that tin foil."

"Yes, ma'am." Becky could almost hear the groan of those in the waiting room, some who'd probably been sitting there hours waiting for someone to diagnose their runny nose or have a doctor explain that a tummy ache wasn't always an emergency. Having worked years in the medical field, she knew how people abused the medical system in Canada. Socialized care meant accessing free emergency care. It also meant people misused it for the silliest of symptoms, which, in turn, increased the wait time for everyone.

The unenviable job of the triage nurse was to prioritize the cases that arrived. Copious bleeding and heart attacks? Those got seen first. Need a few stitches, running a light fever, able to argue your case? Those got to sit while the true emergencies got dealt with.

The tin foil hobo fell under possible emergency, given he was glowing, which indicated he'd probably ingested something he shouldn't. Another reason to put him in a room was because she doubted if they planted his butt in a chair he'd stay there quietly—and Jenny was right about vermin. They didn't want to have to fumigate the emergency room again.

Jenny pointed down the hall. "Cubicle nine is that way."

"Let's go, bud." The scarred older officer bravely put his hand on the shoulder of the shuddering hobo.

Who didn't budge.

"You heard the nice lady. There's a room waiting for you. Food, too, if you behave."

A violent shake of his head was the reply, with dirty fingers reaching up to hold his hat in place.

"You ain't got a choice. Let's go." The cops reached down and grabbed hold of an arm each, then half carried, half dragged the man into a small room. The hobo keened the whole way.

When he refused to stand on his own two feet, the officers hefted him onto the bed. She half expected him to leap off and run. Instead he slumped and whimpered. Poor guy.

The cop with the scar hesitated before leaving. "You got someone else coming to help you?"

"Not with the latest budgets cuts," Becky quipped. "Don't worry. I'll be fine." Having worked the emergency room for a few years now, she'd dealt with her fair share of strange individuals. This one actually seemed more docile than most who arrived in the grips of a drug-induced high. Still, despite his subdued appearance, Becky left the door open.

She faced him and smiled. "My name is Becky. And you are?"

Silence met her cheerful attempt. Becky laid the clipboard on the small counter running along the wall. It held a box with gloves, a plastic jar with cotton swabs, and not much else.

In the small confines of the room, the stench rolling off the hobo proved pungent. Turning partially away, she kept an eye on him while dipping her hand into her pocket. The container of Vaseline had an easy lid to pop open, which meant she could smear some on her finger. She rubbed the cream under her nose, making the odor manageable. Then she snapped a pair of latex gloves on.

During that time, the hobo didn't move.

She wetted some paper napkins, the large sturdy kind, and started with the hands clasped on his knees. He didn't react as she cleaned the surface dirt from him. Not exactly what the triage nurse ordered, but Becky wanted to start slow. Show the man she meant him no harm.

When some of his tension eased, she said softly, "Can you tell me your name?"

To her surprise, he replied. "Doubleu-effninetytwo."

He said it quickly, and she frowned. It almost sounded like he'd said WF92. Which was obviously gibberish, but gibberish that appeared English.

She kept wiping at his hands, noticing the abrasions on them, the engrained dirt. "Do you know where you live?"

"No home." That emerged clear as a bell.

Dumping the paper towel, she decided to tackle the foil next. Seeing a rip in the metal sheathing around his forearm, she tugged at it, the aluminum ripping easily.

He didn't like it. "No." Said with a violent shake of his head as he reached to grab the foil from her.

She crumpled it and put it in the garbage pail at her back. Then, because he seemed to be more inclined to speak, again asked, "What is your name?" Before he could react, she tore the aluminum covering his chest.

No reply other than a shudder. With his tin foil gone, she got treated to the ragged state of his clothes.

Track pants that might have once been blue. A plaid shirt over a dirty cotton tee. All of it beyond repair.

"I'm going to strip you and give you something clean to wear."

He sat there, a breathing rag doll who allowed her to strip him and dress him in a gown open at the back.

She kept up a constant chatter with him, explaining what she was doing, not that he replied. However, his shuddering did ease, his whole body slumped, and she noted that the glow in his eyes was gone.

She made a note on his chart. Eyes: brown. Age: unknown. Hard to tell with the layer of filth on him and the scraggly nature of his hair. He appeared gaunt. Undernourished. His skin pulled taut over bone and muscle.

"You poor thing," she cooed. "Looks like you haven't had a proper meal in ages. The kitchen is closed right now, but I'll see if I can scrounge you up something once I'm done."

He said nothing, but he did lift his head and peek at her.

"Do you know where you are?" Becky asked.

"The bad place."

The reply startled her. "Not bad. You're in a hospital."

"No. No. No. Bad place." The man's wild eyes darted from side to side, and agitation had his body rocking.

"Sir, I need you to remain calm."

"Out. I need out."

"Soon. First, we need to make sure you're okay. Did you take any drugs?" She spoke in a low soothing tone.

"So many drugs," the man cackled.

"Can you give me a name?"

"No name. Noooo name," he sang, still rocking.

"Where did you get the drugs?"

"The bad place." His voice dropped an octave.

The reply made her wonder if he'd escaped from a care facility. It would make sense, a place that gave him drugs, his fear of hospitals.

"Is there someone I can call?"

"No. No. I need my shield. Give it back." He lunged off the table, and his hands dug into the garbage bin. He emerged with his tin foil hat, which he plopped on his head. "Now they can't see me."

Definitely some kind of mental imbalance happening. And maybe something else. The strange light in his eyes had returned, a golden hue most unnatural.

"Sir, can you tell me what drugs you might have taken?" She knew of nothing that could make someone glow. In the movies, it usually meant something radioactive. She sure as hell hoped not. She had enough problems already.

"Not me. Bad. Drugs bad," the man keened as he rocked on the balls of his feet, his skinny legs poking out of the bottom of his gown. "Hurts."

"Where does it hurt?" She'd seen no obvious wounds when she stripped him.

"Hurts everywhere."

"Did someone hurt you?" She guided him to the edge of the bed again, and he sat.

"Yesss." The word spilled from him. "Chimera. Chimera did this." The guy leaned forward suddenly, his eyes wide, and beyond the glow she noticed the iris. His very strange, vertically slitted iris.

"Can you hold still? I'd like to check something." She grabbed a penlight from her pocket and flicked it on. She raised it to shine it in the man's eye.

The man hissed. "No doctors!"

"I'm a nurse."

"No. No Not again." The hobo shrieked again as he lunged for her, his hands reaching for her neck, the tips of his fingers sharp, his nails unshorn and long.

"Help," she squeaked. She hit the cabinet behind her and grabbed at his wrists, doing her best to keep him from crushing her windpipe. Not that it did much good. The transient appeared intent on choking her to death.

Spots danced in front of her eyes. She opened her mouth for a breath, only she couldn't get any air.

Was this how it ended? Not wasting away in a hospital bed but a victim of her work?

She heard shouts. The pounding of feet. And still the pressure continued despite her best efforts to pry him loose.

"Let her go, asshole." The deep voice wasn't one she recognized, but she welcomed it, especially since the fingers around her neck were suddenly gone. She hit the floor on her knees, gasping and choking, her neck throbbing.

Glancing up through streaming eyes, she saw a tall man, dressed in black. His hair dark, the gaze he sent her way even darker.

"Thank you." The words never made a sound even though her lips moved.

"You never saw me," snapped the man before he frog-marched the screaming hobo out of the room. Screams that faded as she remained on her knees, sucking in air.

Only moments later, Jenny and Dr. Morrison entered. Made a fuss over her. Exclaimed about the attack. Declared her bruised but okay. Becky didn't feel okay. She could barely swallow, the pain of the swollen tissue too intense for mere acetaminophen.

The hospital sent her home early—with a prescription for some stronger pain meds—and she was told to take a few days rest with pay.

The pay part she didn't mind; however, sticking close to home wasn't much fun. Watching television didn't help her ignore the fact she could speak only in a hoarse voice and swallowing hurt. She went to the store for ice-cold Popsicles, only to have the cashier gasp when she saw Becky's neck.

Probably should have worn a scarf to hide the crescent moons and bruises marring her flesh. The pamphlet the woman pulled from the behind the desk with info for battered women went into the recycling bin.

She lasted a whole day bored at home before she asked to be put back on the schedule. After all, she'd worked with worse.

Since they were understaffed, no one argued with her demand. She came in to work to discover the hobo who'd attacked her gone.

"Did someone claim him?" she asked, her voice raspy, her throat raw.

"Yeah. The dude who saved you," Eugenia, another nurse on her shift, confided.

"You mean tall, dark, and handsome?" She might

have only caught a glimpse, but he made an impression. "Who was he?"

"No idea. He showed up just in time to save you, from what I hear. Then, not long after, a pair of suits arrived, along with some more big dudes in black military fatigues. They took our John Doe away in a huge SUV."

"No way." How exciting, and she'd missed it. "Do we know why?"

Eugenia shrugged. "No idea. They didn't say shit, but they took everything. His file. The garbage can. Jerry down in security said they even took the camera footage."

It didn't take a journalistic mindset to see the cover-up. What she didn't have were all the details. But a good reporter didn't care if she had to dig.

I smell a story.

CHAPTER TWO

The new rental didn't smell. Thank fuck. With the potent stench his cargo left behind, the one he'd returned would probably get smacked with a cleaning fee.

Not his problem. The company would pay it.

Turning down the radio, Jett watched as the helicopter lifted—cargo safely inside, hog-tied and gagged to ensure a quiet trip—before dialing the secure line to his boss. "Sir, the patient is en route back to the clinic."

"What about the trail he left at the hospital and the law enforcement officials who brought him in?" the voice on the other end asked.

"The trail was wiped." All video footage and written records destroyed. "The only thing we can't remove are the memories of those who saw him."

Although Jett would wager if such a thing existed, he'd be expected to use it. The Chimaeram Clinic held tight to its secrets. He wondered how long before they equipped him with a device a la *Men in Black* to wipe people's recollections.

"Did anyone see anything they shouldn't have?"

How about the fact the general public encountered a clinic patient at all? "The subject didn't exhibit any outward feral signs other than the eyes." A lucky break given some of the clinic's less successful subjects looked more beast than man.

"Stupid side effect," the man on the other end grumbled. "Will any of those who noticed the glowing talk?"

In other words, did they need to do more cleanup? Maybe arrange a car accident. Cause a sudden heart attack.

"Not likely, sir. The cops and the hospital staff assumed he was partaking of drugs."

"What of the nurse he attacked?"

The nurse who almost died? Another minute and Jett wouldn't have arrived in time. Good thing she'd removed the aluminum shielding the target or Jett would have never homed in on his location in time.

The tech guys were working on a better tracking device, one not hampered by metal or easily blitzed with the application of electricity. They'd lost a few targets because of shitty devices.

At least his hunt was over. Target located, and on his way back to the clinic. As to witnesses...

"The nurse is recovering. Surveillance of her phone and internet activity hasn't shown her doing anything suspicious."

"Do we know if the subject told her anything?"

Jett shrugged, despite knowing his boss couldn't see it. "No idea. They were alone for a few minutes before the attack." Time enough for many things to be said. The question was, would the nurse chalk it up as the ramblings of an addict?

"He laid hands on her." A statement that showed his boss had actually read the report.

"Yes."

"Did he draw blood?"

"No." Not that it mattered. What the subject had couldn't be transmitted so easily.

"What of the officers?"

He'd had a drink with them the night before, plying them with shots and joking with them good ol' boy style. They'd discussed some of the many weird cases they encountered, but his target only received a nominal mention in passing as a crazy dude with glowing eyes. "The cops chalked it up to some new drug on the street."

"Might not be a bad idea to release a street drug that will create a few more cases so this one doesn't stand out. That said, I'm still worried about the nurse."

"You want me to stick around and keep an eye on her?" Jett offered. He wasn't in a hurry to enclose himself within the clinic. There was isolation, and then there was his usual place of work. It took a helicopter to get in. Not always the case, but after the first time a patient escaped using one of their trucks, his boss had the passage between the Rocky Mountains sealed. No one ever suspected the avalanche of rocks and dirt was anything but nature made.

"Things are quiet for the moment so, yes, stay in the city a few more days. While you're there, I want you to compile a report for me. I want to know every-thing about this nurse. It could be that she might solve two problems at once."

"On it." Jett hung up with his boss and turned immediately to his laptop. Some folks might have had a problem digging into the life of a civilian, someone innocent of anything but being in the wrong place or time.

Not Jett. He didn't let a petty thing like laws or morals get in his way. He had a job to do. A job that paid him stupidly well. And if it meant digging into the life of a nurse who had the most awful picture on her driver's license, then so be it.

Despite saving her life, he didn't care about her. Didn't give a shit about anyone but himself. She was just a job. A cute one, with the biggest damned eyes and auburn hair that surely came from a bottle.

Funny how he remembered how she looked. It had only been the briefest of glimpses, and yet, as he delved into her life, uncovering her lack of familial attachments, her single status—which he discovered via social media—and her love for ice cream—that repeated credit card charges revealed—he found himself replaying that moment.

That moment where he saved her life—and didn't stick around for the thank-you.

His job wasn't about thanks. Nor could he shirk it because of some big eyes and full lips that a man wouldn't mind touching certain parts of his body.

The boss wanted to know more about her. So Jett staked out her apartment, which proved boring—and fattening. The coffeeshop across from it made some evil good sandwiches and frothy coffee. He followed her to the hospital, noticing no sign of dark or even light roots, despite her red hair pulled back in a tight ponytail. She had true pale skin dotted with freckles. The scrubs she chose to wear to work were loose and light blue in color. Off duty, she usually sported jeans or comfortable athletic wear.

On her time off she did nothing.

Like seriously fucking nothing. She went to work. She went home. She didn't stop for a drink. The wildest she got was popping into the corner store to grab a carton of ice cream. Which she ate alone because no one visited her.

After three days, Jett might have reported all was well and returned to the clinic if she'd not done a Google search that pinged his phone that night. Once he saw what she'd typed in, he cursed and then called his boss.

"We might have a problem."

CHAPTER THREE

The bruises had faded, but the experience remained with Becky. From the way the John Doe totally turned psychotic to his freaky lantern eyes. Add in the way he'd been practically abducted from the hospital and all trace of his presence scrubbed, she found herself curious. Especially about the mysterious guy who'd saved her. Who was he and that group of men who had smuggled John Doe away?

The journalist in her smelled a story. However, she had no way of developing it because she had nothing to go on.

She never did learn John Doe's real name. Despite the suspicion he'd taken some kind of new drug, no one else presented themselves at the hospital emergency with strange glowing eyes. Nor did the rumor mill mention any other cases.

Becky didn't have a single lead. Nothing but a name.

Chimera.

Which, as it turned out, was a ridiculously common term. It could either mean a mythological creature with the head of a lion, tail of a snake, breathing fire, with wings. Or was used in conjunction with science fiction stories of doctors experimenting with hybridizing humans. There were even modern medical applications of the term that indicated the melding of genetics of more than one species.

Crazy stuff. Impossible she would even say, until she remembered the man's eyes. His oh-so-strange eyes. One would almost say inhuman. But saying that aloud would get a nurse placed on leave and talking to someone while lying on a couch. *"Yes, my childhood sucked. No, I don't have mommy or auntie issues. He really did look like he was dipped in a vat of radioactive stuff."*

There were pills for people who made those kinds of claims.

Besides, talking about it meant bringing in more people on the mystery. She kind of wanted to keep her suspicions to herself. Crack this nut. Claim all the fame.

It was possible the entire event was benign. But looking into it, spinning wild stories in her mind, helped her to ignore the ache under her ribs. The tickle in her throat.

After the failed attempt at finding something about Chimera, she spent time on the internet doing more searches, such as reasons why a man's eyes might glow. More than one comic book series pointed her toward radiation and super powers.

She tried researching Chimera locally, trying to see if perhaps there was a lab practicing the so-called melding of genetics. She even typed in WF92, which turned out to be a miniature spy cam.

Everything led to a dead end. Her one chance at a scoop and she'd screwed it up by almost being choked to death, getting sent home, and missing the excitement.

Bummer.

The next day, as she sorted laundry before going to work, a knock at her door brought a frown to her brow. She lived in a secure building that required people to be buzzed in. She pressed her eye to the peephole and found herself even further confused by the stranger standing in the hall wearing a suit.

"Can I help you?" she asked loud enough to be heard. No way was she opening the door. Safety first.

"I'm looking for a Miss Frederickson."

Her heart stuttered. "Why?"

"She recently took care of a patient."

"She's a nurse. She sees lots of people."

"This one behaved most inappropriately. We wanted to thank her for not pressing charges."

He could only be referring to one person. Throwing caution out the window, she opened the door. "You know John Doe?"

"Actually, his name is Seymour. And yes, I know him. He's a patient at the clinic I work for. We were quite perturbed when he went missing."

"He escaped your clinic?" Which totally made a bunch of things he said take on a new light.

"Yes and gave us all quite the scare considering he was gone for months. It's a miracle Seymour survived with his condition."

"What's wrong with him?"

The man in the suit tapped his temple. "Tumor. It's addled his wits I'm afraid."

"Is that why he tried to kill me?" she asked bluntly.

"A regrettable incident. And one of the reasons why I'm here. May I come in?" He angled his head and dangled a briefcase.

Since she highly doubted he was here to murder her, she stepped aside and opened the door wide in invitation. The man entered, and she noticed the nice cut of his suit, his hair perfectly trimmed, and the cologne, which tickled her nose.

He appeared in his late forties, maybe older. Hard to tell, as he appeared fit. But his silver temples indicated some age, as did the faint crease lines by his mouth. The small round glasses were a nice touch, and she wondered if they were prescription or part of his look.

The man set his briefcase on the kitchen table before turning to her with a smile. "I've been remiss. Excuse my poor manners. I never did introduce myself. I'm Gary Lowry, legal counsel for the Chimaeram Clinic."

She'd never heard of it. "You're a lawyer?"

"Yes. Although I only handle the one client."

"And you're here to what? Make sure I don't sue?" Not that Becky knew what she'd sue for. Hardly the clinic's fault if a patient escaped and acted out. Working emergency meant her contract stated she wouldn't take legal action against patients who often behaved outside the accepted norms.

"The incident with Seymour was regrettable. In apology, I've been instructed to give you this." He opened his briefcase and pulled out an envelope. He held it out. "This is for you."

"What is it?"

"A check along with a form indemnifying us from legal action."

A peek inside the envelope showed a check with many zeros. Too many. She handed it back. "I can't accept this." Mostly because, if she did, then this curious case would never go to print.

"I can inquire about increasing the amount."

"What? No. I mean it's too much and for something that wasn't a big deal. We get people high on meth and other stuff all the time. Sometimes they get violent. It's just part of the job."

"And a remarkable job it is. Which is why I insist you take it." He pressed it into her hand and then said, "I don't suppose you'd be interested in changing employers?"

"Why?"

"The clinic is looking to hire a few nurses. It would be for a six-month contract, available for extension if it works out. We provide everything you need: housing, food, entertainment, plus a highly competitive paycheck."

"How competitive?"

She blinked when he told her. "That's awfully

generous." Also, way more than she was making working at the hospital.

"Given the remote location of our clinic, we feel it's a required enticement."

"How remote are we talking?"

"Once inside the clinic, you're there for the six-month duration."

"So no visits to town, even for a movie?"

Lowry shook his head. "There are no roads to drive on. All supplies and personnel come in via helicopter. Which might sound daunting, however, as mentioned, we provide everything a person might possibly need."

The more he spoke, the more he piqued her intrigue. A hidden clinic paying ridiculous amounts for staff who treated a dude with glowing eyes?

She totally wanted to do it. Her throat itched, and she couldn't help a small cough.

It was a reminder of why she couldn't go far. Her elation deflated, as if pricked by a needle.

"I can't."

Mr. Lowry arched a brow. "Can't? You have a commitment keeping you here?"

"Well, there is my place." Her less than awesome apartment filled with an eclectic assortment of furniture and knickknacks.

"We can ensure your rent and utilities are paid for the duration of your stay."

The man appeared determined to make it impossible to refuse. Still...with her problem. He'd said it himself. No way out.

Then again, there wasn't much they could do here either. So why was she refusing? This might be her last and only chance to find the story she'd been waiting for.

"Where do I sign up?"

The actual terms of her employment took two hours of paperwork. So many questions.

Names of her parents. Siblings. The fact she had no living family made that part quick; the aunt who raised her had died of cancer. She was stumped by emergency contact. Her best friend had just taken a job in Panama. Other friends had moved on with their lives, getting married, having kids, meaning their interests diverged, and they didn't remain in contact.

Everyone else she knew was just an acquaintance. Becky might be outgoing, but she didn't make friends easily.

Criminal background check. They'd find nothing. Not even a parking ticket.

Next section: health. There she hesitated again, and Lowry noticed.

"Something the matter?"

"Yes. I have a problem breathing sometimes." Understatement.

"Then you should jump at this opportunity. Fresh mountain air outside. Perfectly clean oxygen inside. Plus, state-of-the-art machinery to help you breathe should you have an asthma attack."

He misunderstood, and she couldn't in good faith lie. "I'm in remission. For cancer," she expanded.

"What kind?" he asked.

"Lung." And then, because she was used to the look people gave her, quickly added, "I don't smoke. Never have. But my aunt did. She raised me. Always had a cigarette in her mouth." Dangling from her lip as she cooked over the stove. Ashing the burning tube in an overflowing tray as she helped Becky muddle with homework. "I got lung cancer by the time I was in my early twenties. They removed part of my left lung and, with chemo, managed to prevent other tumors from growing." Her aunt wasn't so lucky. She lost the battle.

"But you're in remission currently?"

She nodded. The pain in her chest might be due to all kinds of things. Probably nothing, but just in case, she'd gone for an MRI just before the attack. The results were pending.

"Will mountain air affect your ability to work?"

"No." She laughed. "Fresh air is actually good for me."

"Then I see no issue with it. We wouldn't be a very caring clinic if we held your past health problems against you."

With that issue out of the way, it was back to reading more pages of legal jargon. Including the actual contract stating the terms of her employment. Then came the non-disclosure stuff.

Becky eyed the thick document. "Wow. Exactly what are you guys doing that requires all this?"

"This is more standard than you think with medical institutes that also have research aspects. Company secrets have to be protected."

"Does this mean you're going to take our cell phones when we arrive?" she joked.

"No need since there's no cell signal."

The reply stole her voice for a second. "So no phone calls to the outside world?"

"All employees are set up with terminals that are attached to the internet, giving Skype abilities as well as email access."

"But let me guess, your company will read the mail and listen in to make sure we're not spilling secrets."

A small smile curved his lips. "Not actual people

but an AI system that is programmed to flag certain words."

Hard core stuff out of a movie or a book, which only made her more determined to take the job.

When all the i's were dotted and the t's crossed, Lowry tucked the documents into his briefcase. "That takes care of all of it."

"When do I start?" she asked.

"Is one week too soon?"

Not soon enough. Especially when her doctor called her the next day with devastating news.

CHAPTER FOUR

Peering at the monitor, Jett frowned. There was the new nurse. The same one he'd saved at the hospital and had yet to actually meet.

A meeting that wouldn't happen anytime soon since he watched her on a screen, which wasn't some creepy way of stalking her. At his boss's request, he was monitoring shit. AKA making sure the employees behaved. During his routine work, he happened to notice her.

Her bright smile—which tugged at his grumpy lips.

Trim figure—which tugged him below the belt.

Gullible countenance—that made a man want to shake her and ask her what she was thinking.

Jett had been around long enough to know she wasn't hired just because of her credentials. Chimera wanted Nurse Frederickson, Becky of the glossy red hair. Wanted her not because she'd seen and heard too much. Not because she knew how to draw blood or take a temperature. The head doctor saw her as a tool. A means to an end.

Jett's job was to ensure she didn't get away. Which, given their seclusion in the mountains, didn't seem likely, and yet Chimera had assigned him the task of watching over her. Especially once he learned of her journalistic attempts.

"I don't need her spouting off to some newspaper about the secret clinic in the Rockies," Chimera ranted.

"Then throw her in a cell on level six."

"I'm thinking about it," Chimera muttered.

"If you're that worried about her blabbing, then cut off her internet access. Blame it on some techy problem."

"I'm surprised you're not suggesting a more obvious solution," Chimera taunted in that sly way he had.

Kill the girl? *"You want her gone, then say the word."* He knew it was the right answer, the only answer, so why did he feel a wrenching in his gut?

"I just might. You're a good company man," his boss praised.

No, he was a man who didn't give a shit what

others did so long as it didn't affect him or his bottom line. One woman with a quirky smile wasn't worth causing shit over. He told himself that and, yet, couldn't quite shake an unsettled feeling.

A few days later, taken off the employee stalking roster and put on a floor shift, Jett ran into the new nurse, or rather she ran into him.

Literally.

She emerged from a room as he patrolled the corridors, keeping an eye out for wandering patients and personnel in the wrong spot. One of the many jobs he had. Chimera's paranoia convinced him that everyone wanted to steal from him. Wanted to take his work and claim the glory.

The doctor wasn't entirely wrong. Why just last month Jett had to take a certain guard to level six. The pussy blubbered the entire way. Claimed he did it for his family.

Didn't matter the reason. The man betrayed the clinic. Chimera took issue with it. Jett provided the solution. The animal attack left the guard in pieces, which was why the boss was gracious enough to pay for the funeral and provided extended benefits to the man's surviving family.

Which was a hell of a lot more than Jett would have done for a traitor.

Traitors weren't the only things he sometimes

dealt with. When patients escaped, he got to play the part of hunter. Couldn't let the public know about what the clinic did. They wouldn't understand.

That day, Jett played the part of regular guard, assigned hall duty on boring level four. The level where the patients slept. An easy enough task. Not really. Only an idiot would relax in this place.

When he'd hired on two years ago, Jett had not truly grasped what they were doing. On the surface, the Chimaeram Clinic seemed kosher, if somewhat psycho about security and privacy. Then he began to see things—things that didn't make sense outside of a horror movie. He heard things—whispers, partial statements. It didn't take a genius to put two and two together. The clinic was playing in some very gray areas. Areas supposedly forbidden in the medical world.

A more up-and-up guy might have blown a whistle.

Jett wasn't that guy. Especially since he could see the good they were trying to do. The clinic was involved in some cutting-edge shit. Shit that took cripples and helped them walk again. People dying of cancer and other horrible shit, cured. Not just in remission but fucking cured.

His own ma could have used that. She'd died

when he was little. Breast cancer. Which meant he was left alone with his dad.

Cancer killed in more ways than one.

Of course, as with many treatments, there were some side effects. Craziness, which the doctors termed a loss of mental cognition. Violence, as some of those medicated turned feral and animal-like. Even some physical oddities that no amount of plastic surgery would fix.

But Jett ignored the fact the doctors experimented on humans, firstly because every single one of these patients had volunteered and, secondly, he was paid to keep his mouth shut.

Paid well. Plus fed. And he got to shoot things when the demons inside his head got to be a little too much.

Jett wasn't what you'd call a nice fellow. The only reason he wasn't in jail was because he'd joined the military at eighteen. They had a use for guys like him. Dispatched overseas, he worked out his aggressive tendencies killing shit. Enjoyed it a little too much and got discharged.

Blow up one wrong house and the higher-ups got mad. Never mind how many they accidentally killed by friendly fire. Or the fact that his superior gave him the wrong address. Jett became their fall guy.

He was released upon the world without a

purpose. So he gave himself one. Modelled himself off that Dexter dude on television. But eventually he slipped up and the cops brought Jett in for questioning—and some out-of-sight high fives—which was when Lowry found him and offered him a job. As Lowry explained, the clinic wanted guys who weren't afraid to act—and didn't have a problem ignoring the laws.

Jett's reply? *I am your man.* Who would have thought Jett would become a dedicated company man? Most times he loved his job.

Most times.

He did, however, hate his assigned rotations to level four. Level four was for those still sleeping as the drugs were pumped into their systems. Supposedly the comas were induced because, otherwise, the people being cured whined. Healing apparently hurt.

Why a guard for coma patients, though, you might wonder?

Because when they woke up, not all of them were thankful and nurses were not easy to replace. Not good ones at least. Chimaeram had very specific needs when it came to staff. No attachments preferred.

Lowry preferred to head hunt those with no close family or friends. There tended to be fewer questions asked if the nurse didn't return after her six-month stint.

They had to be of a certain age, the preference being early twenties to mid-thirties. Which Jett never understood. Surely older nurses would be better. Just look at how many of the nurses the clinic hired ended up pregnant.

With little to do, fucking was a favored pastime. Not that Jett indulged. *Don't fuck those you work with.* A mantra he lived by. His hand was good enough when the urge hit, and when he accompanied Lowry on jobs outside the clinic, he satisfied his carnal needs with strangers.

And never looked back.

Which was why he would ignore the woman who ricocheted off his chest as she came bouncing out a door—despite the fact he got hard every time he saw her.

He'd done well thus far. Given he'd been keeping an eye on her, it proved easy to avoid her when she strayed into the communal area for food or entertainment.

Problem was, even though he'd avoided her in person, he'd not been able to stop thinking of her. He knew everything about her, from her fetish for ice cream to the strawberry shampoo she preferred. The way her left cheek dimpled when she laughed. How her ass looked when she bent over—in his dreams, that ass was usually naked.

She squeaked as she lost her balance.

His hand shot out to grab her before she could fall.

"Goodness," she exhaled. "That was close. Thanks for saving me."

Save? Technically he'd done it twice now. Totally out of character. He let go of her as if she suddenly burned.

"You should watch where you're going." Said in his gruffest tone of voice.

She seemed oblivious to the rebuke and smiled at him. "Aren't you just a ray of sunshine this morning."

There was only one thing to do in reply. Scowl.

"Are you today's guard?" she chirped. "I don't think we've met, but you seem awfully familiar."

Maybe because she'd featured in a few of his more X-rated dreams.

"Don't you have work to do?" he asked since she kept grinning at him.

"Indeed, I do. I'm the new nurse."

No shit. Even if he hadn't scouted her for Lowry it would have been obvious. The staff were always easily recognizable, given the owner had a perverse sense of humor. Maintenance wore gray coveralls. Guards, black fatigues. Doctors, the classic white coats, and nurses sported ridiculous little caps with a red cross on their heads. What surprised him was the owners of this place didn't also put them in short, tight dresses.

She'd look good in something like that, especially bent over.

He glared at her, because somehow it had to be her fault that the thought even crossed his mind.

"We both need to get our asses back to work," Jett grumbled.

Did the fool woman listen?

Nope.

"I'm Becky." She held out her hand.

He stared at it. Stared at her. Was she seriously that oblivious? He wasn't interested. Mostly. Kind of.

Fuck.

"Jett." The name slipped past his lips.

She repeated it with candy-coated glossed lips. "Jett. Suits you. All tough and dark and menacing."

Since every word she spoke was the truth, his chest swelled. It only served to deepen his scowl. "Don't think flirting is gonna get you anywhere." He knew the type. Bat her eyelashes, wet her lips, and expect him to do favors. "I'm watching you." More than she knew.

The dimple appeared. "You make it sound so naughty. You been working here long?"

The woman seemed determined to chitchat. Jett didn't chitchat. He ordered people to do their job. Hell, he should be doing his job, making the rounds. Looking and listening for trouble. The coma ward was the most deceiving of the places they had to patrol. The patients lulled everyone into a false sense of security with their deep sleep. But when they woke up... Full-on chaotic meltdown.

Totally awesome. For him at any rate. Others? Not so much.

Jett had once asked Dr. Chimera after an incident why they didn't strap them all down. Apparently, it made the nurses' work more difficult what with them having to flip the patients around to massage them and do their other tasks. Compared to the doctors and scientists, nurses were expendable in the grand scheme of things, which Jett wasn't entirely comfortable with, but hey, he was paid to not care.

Before he could bark at the new nurse to stop being a lazy ass, she bobbed her head, the jaunty cap distracting, and chirped, "See you later, Jett."

Not likely.

She slapped her card on a reader and bounced into another room, leaving him alone in the hall. A hall he'd already walked once. Yet chose to saunter down again. He'd just finished his second cursory check when he heard her call for him.

"Oh, Jett." Spoken in a singsong voice. He glanced back down the corridor, noting her head peeking out from the first door, her cap pointing the way.

"What?"

"Can you give me a hand?"

He knew where he'd like to give her his hand. She might even agree to it. But he was on the company clock.

"I'm kind of busy."

"Yes, I can see you are. All that stomping around, glaring at stuff. Very busy indeed. This will just take a second."

"Is there a problem?" he asked, his steps clomping even louder as he neared her. He did not glare. He stared around with suspicion.

"Yes. The bed seems to be jammed. I need some muscle to help me get it to move."

There wasn't a man alive who didn't get a swagger when a little woman asked for help.

He was no exception. Entering the room, she showed him the dilemma. The sheet had somehow gotten wedged in the mechanism that allowed the bed to change position.

With a little ripping and colorful swearing, he managed to free it, and the nurse clapped her hands.

"My hero."

The use of the word "hero" threw him. No one had ever called him that before. Bastard, asshole, the cum his mother should have swallowed. But never the good guy.

It made him feel warm in a way he didn't like, which, in turn, brought a frown to his brow.

But she didn't cower under his stern gaze.

She smiled. "Thank you." Then she turned her back on him and went to work.

Whereas he stupidly stared for a minute, maybe longer than he should have, as she bent over displaying a pert, round ass.

A man could grab hold of those curvy hips and slam into that tight—

Whoa.

Jett did an abrupt about-face and exited the room. No dirty thoughts about the staff. She was cute, but not worth the hassle. Last thing he needed was to give in to lust, bang her, and then have her giving him big cow eyes every time he saw her. Because he wasn't the type to go back for seconds. It just encouraged women to be clingy.

As his shift finished, he had the mischance of bumping into her again.

He had to wonder if she did it on purpose, given how she flew out of the last room and once again slammed into him.

This time he didn't grab hold of her.

She reached for him. And held on.

Smiled up at him.

Winked.

Winked in a way that made him harden.

Then sauntered away without saying a word, leaving him staring after her.

And that night, she was once again in his dreams. Wearing a short little dress.

Her ass was just as nice as he'd hoped.

CHAPTER FIVE

As the weeks passed, Becky's frustration grew. She had yet to solve the mystery of the Chimaeram Clinic. Not for lack of trying. The people working in this place were a tight-lipped bunch. She'd not made many friends among the nurses. Mostly because of a language barrier with several of them. It would seem Mr. Lowry didn't just hire local. About the only woman friend she had was Margaret, who was standoffish at best and always changed the subject when she tried to talk about their job.

A job that was boooooooring. Coma patients didn't do a thing but sleep. All day. All the time. Becky spent her work shifts flipping, massaging, checking IVs, taking blood, and emptying bodily waste bags. Sponge baths were also part of it, and at first she blushed mightily when she had to wash around the male parts of her patients.

Good-looking guys she should add. The girls, too. She had no idea of their names. The tablet with her daily instructions didn't say much. It referred to them by a letter and number. Each one slightly different, just like their IVs differed.

Since she found the labels impersonal, she'd given them names. Pixie, petite, and perfect, her rosebud mouth waiting for true love's kiss to wake her. Larry, a more brutish fellow with a Hispanic cast to his features and thick, silky black hair. JR, a big handsome fellow with short-cropped hair who could have been the twin of that character in *Duke Nukem*. Then there was Pixie, with the uncanny purple eyes. She'd opened them once while Becky was washing her.

Scared the shit out of her, especially since she did nothing else.

Almost a month here, and none of her patients had woken up, not on her watch anyhow, yet she arrived one morning to find JR missing and his room wiped clean.

The only person she had to ask about it was Mr. McSurly. The man was always around, usually sporting a scowl. At first, she thought it was his work face, and yet, the few times she saw him in the common area, he glared. For some reason he'd taken an instant dislike to her. Which kind of sucked because he was hot, in a dark and probably a serial-killer-in-his-spare-time kind of way.

His attitude usually would put him in the not-her-type category, yet despite all the other guards in this place that flirted with her, there was only one she wished would smile her way. The best she'd managed was a disgusted sigh when she tripped yet again over her own two feet.

She didn't let his apparent dislike of her person deter her from being friendly when she ran into him in the hall. Not actually into him this time. She managed to walk and smile at the same time, which was harder than it sounded. The man had the ability to unsettle her.

"Hey there, Jett. How's it been hanging?" She would say at least eight inches, more than a hand thick and slightly to the right.

"Don't you have somewhere to be?"

"As a matter of fact, I do," she said. "But funny thing, the patient is missing. Do you know what happened to JR?"

"Who the fuck is JR? And why the fuck would I know?"

"JR was the guy sleeping in this room." She jabbed a finger at the door. "He's gone."

The big guard shrugged. "Probably woke up and got moved."

"To level five?"

"Don't know. Don't care."

"Well I do," she huffed. She was possibly the only one who did, and did those snooty nurses on level five care? Nope. They wouldn't tell her anything. They had a cone of silence that no amount of cheerful banter would break.

Becky hadn't quite reached the point of despair when it came to breaking the story she knew hid in this place, but at times she wanted to scream in frustration. An impatience fueled by the almost constant tickle in her lungs.

Just a cold. People got them all the time. Never mind what the MRI said.

"You're not paid to care," he retorted.

"That seems cold."

"Listen, you seem like a nice girl, so let me give you a piece of advice. Do your job."

"I am doing my job." Spoken with an indignant note.

"No, you're not. You think it hasn't been noticed you're asking questions? Lots of them."

How did he know? She thought she'd been discreet. "Curiosity is healthy."

"It also killed the fucking cat."

She rolled her eyes. "Why must it always be doom and gloom with you?"

"Always?" He snorted. "Seems like a rather broad statement given we barely know each other."

"And whose fault is that?" The sassy reply actually snapped his mouth shut.

Not for long. "What is your problem?"

"You are my problem. You and that perpetual scowl. Would it kill you to be nice once in awhile? Maybe even try a grin, or has it been so long you're afraid it will hurt?" Yes, she threw down a challenge. She just couldn't help herself.

His lips pulled apart, the smile cold, and yet somehow sexy. "I know how to smile. But only for people I like."

Oooh. Definite dig. "Why don't you like me?" For some reason it seemed important to find out. Every other guy in this place panted after her. Not Jett. Problem was she saw him watching her all the time. She'd enter a room, and his gaze would zero in on her. Or she'd feel that prickle between her shoulder blades, and when she turned, she'd find him walking away.

It wasn't her imagination or conceit that made

her believe he found her attractive. And yet he seemed determined to be a dick and push her away.

"Why the fuck do you care if I like you?"

Good question. "We have to work together."

"No. You have to work in that room." He jabbed a finger at a closed door. "I make sure no one throttles you while you do it."

Her hand went to her neck, his words reminding her of the incident a month ago in the hospital. "How would you even know if I needed help? It's not like you're in the room with me when I'm dealing with a patient."

"I'd know." He patted his hip, indicating the hand-held unit clipped there. "Someone is always watching. And listening." The last sounding like a warning before he turned on his heel and strode away, the clomp of his boots as expressive as his scowl.

She stuck out her tongue. Jerk. He obviously couldn't help himself. Just like she couldn't help finding him interesting.

That afternoon she started her shift by checking on Larry—what she'd named the beak-nosed guy in room four oh four. She'd noticed him sweating earlier, which seemed odd given the rooms were climate controlled and he didn't run a fever.

Entering his room—which had much in common

with a cell given the sparseness of it, bed, a few pieces of equipment, and nothing else, not even a bright picture to liven up the space—the first thing she noticed was how still her patient appeared. Usually she could see his chest rising and falling. Not only did nothing move, she didn't hear him breathing either.

"Oh dear." She rushed to Larry's side and put her hand to his chest, exhaling in relief at the steady thump of his heart. "Naughty boy, giving me a scare," she chided. She noted the clammy sweat of earlier was gone. His skin appeared dry, and a press of the back of her hand against his forehead showed his temperature normal. Not the most scientific method, but experience with fevers meant she could tell by touch.

"Let's check your vitals, shall we," she chirped as she turned around to grab a few things. She had the tendency to talk to the patients. Mostly nonsense chatter about her day, the antics of the guards, the yummy soup she had for lunch. She didn't know if they could hear but didn't think it would hurt to let them know someone was there, caring for them.

When she turned back around, she uttered a gasp. Larry stared at her, his eyes open wide, the blue irises so pale as to almost be translucent, the pupils, tiny pinpricks of black.

"Well hello there." She smiled. "You're awake. How wonderful."

He said nothing. Didn't even blink. Kind of freaky and just like Pixie had done once before. Probably some kind of muscle reflex. Still, those in charge would want to be informed.

"I should let the doctors know you're conscious."

"No." The low, gruff word slipped past his lips and sent a shiver down her spine.

He really was awake. How wonderful.

"You don't want me to get them yet? I can understand that," she gushed. "I mean you just woke up, and probably aren't too crazy about having some doctors poke and prod you. How are you feeling?"

"Hu-u-u-n-n-gry." The word rolled out of him and raised goosebumps on her flesh. And was it her, or did his eyes seem to shine a little too bright?

"Hungry? I can fix that. Let me just go grab you something from the cafeteria." She took a step away from the bed, Mr. Lowry's warning suddenly echoing in her head—*If they so much as twitch, you are to notify us immediately. There is a red button. Press it and vacate the room.* Problem was the red button was by the door, on the other side of the bed.

"No." The single syllable emerged stronger this time. However, it was the fact Larry sat up in bed and then pivoted so his legs dangled off the edge that kind of worried her.

How remarkable he could manage it. Most coma patients had muscle atrophy issues and coordination problems as their bodies woke from their long healing slumber.

Not Larry. He braced his hands on the mattress and pushed himself to his feet.

He didn't fall.

Didn't wobble.

And yes, his eyes were definitely freaking glowing, cold ice chips lit from within.

She took another step back. "I really should get a doctor."

"No doctor." A rumbled demand joined by a curled lip.

Utterly spooked, she decided to stop screwing around. Despite knowing it was dumb, she turned her back on Larry and ran for the door.

She didn't make it.

A fist tangled itself in her hair, grabbing hold and yanking her off her feet. Sharp agony stabbed at her scalp. A pained cry escaped her, and her hands went to the grip in a vain attempt to pry it loose.

Larry didn't seem inclined to release Becky. He swung her around, the sharp tug of hair bringing tears to her eyes.

"Please, let go." She wasn't above pleading.

"Hungry," he stated, the syllables thick, the intent menacing.

"I'll get you food."

"You food." The most chilling thing she'd ever heard.

Becky stared at his face, the eyes wide and freaky, his mouth open, and his teeth glistening. Teeth that appeared rather pointed.

And what was wrong with his face?

Having cared for him close to a month, how had she never noticed the odd slope of his forehead, the jut of his lower jaw, and hadn't she shaved him this morning? Yet he sported a thick growth of hair that spread across his face, covering his chin and cheeks and even extending down his neck.

He released her suddenly, and Becky made a dash for freedom, only to find herself falling, the foot he'd extended tripping her.

She hit the floor hard and cried out again. Then, for good measure, let out a piercing scream as he pounced her.

The feeble attempt at struggling did not stop him from flipping her over. He straddled her body, his eyes glowing brighter than ever, his teeth, definitely longer and sharper than before.

He reached for her neck. Grabbed hold. Squeezed.

Despite her mouth being open wide, she couldn't scream. Couldn't make a sound at all or even draw a breath.

Spots danced before her eyes, and she realized in that moment, *I'm going to die.*

CHAPTER SIX

JETT ALMOST DIDN'T HEAR IT. HE WAS ABOUT TO leave Ward D to patrol the next wing when a faint scream, abruptly cut off, caught his attention. He didn't need the crackling walkie-talkie clipped to his belt barking, "Code Red room four oh four," to know he had to move his ass

It took too many seconds for his key card to unlock the door. By the time he entered, Becky's lips were turning blue and her eyelids fluttered shut.

"Oh, hell no, motherfucker. Get your hands off her!" he yelled.

The gun was in his hand without even thinking, and he fired the darts at the patient. One, two, three. Not enough to take the adrenalized guy down, but enough to draw his attention.

The patient released the nurse and came at Jett,

his eyes glowing eerily, his pupils shrunk to only pinpoints. The subject's lips pulled back in a snarl.

Not one to be intimidated, Jett snarled right back. "Get on your knees, asshole." He steadied his weapon, conscious of the fact he had only two darts left. Would it be enough?

"Hungry!" yelled the patient, spittle flying. He lunged, and Jett quickly fired, the darts hitting and having no effect.

As the patient slammed into him, the gun went spinning from his hand. Not that it would do him any good. Jett shoved at the heavy man and swept his foot around his ankle. He didn't manage to topple the patient, but he did gain some time, enough to dance back and set himself into a more defensive position.

Bracing his legs slightly apart, Jett crouched a little, his body loose and limber. "You wanna wrestle? Let's go." With no darts left, he needed to buy time. Those watching would have called reinforcements. He just had to distract the patient—whose strength exceeded his own—and stay alive.

Not for the first time, he cursed the doctors for not using restraints. Part of their trying to make things look normal. Regular hospitals used them only in extreme cases. The clinic counted as extreme in his mind because, while not all those who woke went psychotic, enough did to be an issue. The nurse, lying prone on the floor, who'd yet to twitch since his arrival, would probably agree.

He'd bitch at his bosses later, once the patient was subdued. Right now, he dodged ham-fisted swings. A roundhouse kick got the fellow in the face. He was sure he heard a crack.

The patient didn't even flinch. But it did piss him off. The guy roared. He also got bigger.

And bigger.

His whole body bulged as the muscles expanded, adrenalized and pumped.

Not good.

"Would someone get their fucking ass down here with some more tranquilizers," Jett bellowed as the patient rushed him. He dove under the thrown punch that would have probably broken something if it had landed. At times like these, he really wished they'd arm him with bullets instead of sleeping agents.

Only those outside got to use real guns. The doctors weren't about to see their projects killed because a guard might foolishly value his own life.

The fucker managed to back Jett into a corner, well away from the nurse, with his back to the hallway door.

The patient thought he'd won and grinned. Not

a pretty sight. A face not even a mother would love with a sloping forehead, jutting cheekbones, and a nose that was flattened.

Jett smiled right back and held out his hands. "That's right, you big fucking dummy. Pay attention to me." Because that meant the patient wasn't looking behind him and the guards who came rushing in could fire their darts.

This time, there were enough of them hammering the subject's body that he went down, a surprised look on his face. A face that smashed into the floor with a crunch that probably meant a broken nose. As Jett walked by, he gave the guy a kick. "Get him down to level six," he barked. "And make sure he's tied up tight." Next time the beast awoke, they'd want to avoid an incident.

Speaking of incident, his boss would want him to take care of the dead nurse. He knelt by her, confused by the sadness filling him as he stared at her still body. A body that gave a rattling gasp.

"Shit, she's still alive." He glanced up at the camera watching. "She's not dead. What should I do with her?" Because this close he could see her throat was damaged, possibly crushed beyond normal repair.

Normal for a civilian hospital. But this was the Chimaeram Clinic, where the impossible happened.

The walkie-talkie at his waist crackled. "Bring her to my lab," the big cheese himself replied.

"Right away, sir."

First, though, he should stabilize her neck before he caused more damage. Jett rummaged in the cabinets until he found something to keep her head from wobbling around. The process quickly accomplished yet not fast enough as her breathing grew labored, each inhalation rattled.

"Don't you go dying on me, Red." For some reason the soft words emerged from him, almost as if he cared what happened to her. He should be glad that, for once, she couldn't run her motor mouth. Yet, the apparently sadistic side of him missed her bubbly attitude.

Jett scooped the nurse into his arms and stood, noticing the slightness of her frame. Just a wee thing against a brute. She'd never stood a chance.

Running would jostle her broken neck too much; however, time wasted. Jett walked briskly, his steps loud in the hall, louder than the doctors rushing past him, their chatter excited—"...showing signs of incredible strength." Never mind the fact their test subject tried to kill a woman.

He slipped into the elevator and snapped, "Habitat level."

Because Chimera didn't work amongst the other

doctors. He had his own lab, a secret lab, and only a few knew about it and had access. Exiting the elevator, Becky cradled in his arms, her breathing shallow with long pauses in between the wheezing, he glanced quickly for anyone watching. Seeing no one, he strode straight forward into the section marked "Under Construction," past the curve in the hall that hid him from sight, right to the rock wall at the back.

Usually he would have to press his badge against the hidden console, but Chimera must have been watching. The secret door slid open with only a whisper of sound, and to anyone watching, he would have appeared to walk straight through the rock wall. Holograms hid the entrance.

He entered a hallway, seemingly benign if you ignored the grills running the length of it. Should the wrong sort get this far, the security measures would kick in and, depending on Chimera's mood, either drop the person into a deep sleep or turn them into pink slime with no chance of recovery.

Not a pretty sight he might add. He'd seen it only once, an assistant of Chimera's thinking he could steal secrets and get away with it.

Ned's death served as a lesson to others—and made the monsters in the cages happy at the change in diet.

Looking down at the nurse's face, he could only

hope she wouldn't be dumb enough to tell anyone what she saw. Chimera would fix her and, in doing so, make her part of the secret.

A secret that might kill her as easily as fix her. Not everyone reacted the same to the medicine in this place. Some became better versions than themselves. Others...others got locked away to never see the light of day again. But what choice did he have?

Becky wouldn't survive without special help.

As Jett reached the far end of the hall, he did his best to not react at the sudden hiss. Decontamination was a must if you wanted entry. The gas didn't hurt, but it did ensure no live microbes made it into the inner sanctum.

He stood with his burden until the door opened onto a state-of-the-art lab. Pristine white and glistening clean.

He entered and found Chimera waiting for him. The man wore a white lab coat over his usual preppy clothes, pressed trousers and a collared shirt.

"Put her over here." Chimera pointed, and Jett obeyed, laying her carefully on the bed, noting the pole with its hanging sack of dark liquid ready by its side.

Kyle, Chimera's assistant—who was silent not because of fear if he talked but because he had no vocal cords—rushed to help. He rolled up the woman's sleeve. With deft fingers, he inserted a tube into her arm. The liquid began its drip.

Chimera turned to Jett. "I need you to hold her down while I apply the osseous compound to her neck."

Hold her down because it would hurt, and Chimera obviously didn't think they had time to waste tethering her to the rails. Jett straddled her on the bed, his body pinning her lower half, his hands gripping her shoulders.

Even as Jett positioned himself, Chimera approached with a big fucking needle, the glass vial filled with a bright green fluid. The osseous compound, made specifically to heal bone injuries. Nasty shit that he'd thankfully never needed.

Jett retained a placid expression as the doctor began to poke and inject, the needle sliding into skin already a dark, mottled color.

At the third pinprick, the nurse's eyes opened wide and unseeing. Her lips parted, and she struggled for breath.

Struggled to scream.

Her body arched. Spasmed. Fought against his grip. A bucking pinto and yet Jett held firm. She needed this treatment. Still, he couldn't help but hate the pain he saw gripping her.

His fault. If he'd run faster. Checked sooner. Perhaps she wouldn't be writhing in agony.

Guilt. A new emotion. He didn't understand why here, why now. Nor did he look away when she caught his gaze and held it. Pleading with him.

Begging. He'd seen that look before, the one that said, *I welcome death.* Except, for once, he didn't make the wish come true.

He murmured, "It's all right, Red. It hurts now, but I promise the doctor is gonna make it all better."

Of course, getting better involved more pain first. The osseous compound was a miraculous thing that could heal traumatic injury, like crushed bone and damaged tissue, but there was a cost.

There was always a cost.

Thankfully she lost consciousness as Chimera kept going with his needle until he finally declared, "I think that's enough. Any more and she might go into seizure."

Not to mention the stuff cost a fortune to make. Jett didn't know what the serum was comprised of but knew Chimera only used it sparingly.

"Should I take her to her room?" he asked as he climbed off. He ignored Kyle as he scurried around fastening restraints around her limbs.

"Not yet. I want to observe her for a bit. Take a few x-rays. Make sure there isn't any cranial bleeding. She hit the floor pretty hard when the patient tripped her."

The reminder of her attack had him growling, "And this is why the sleeping subjects should be tied down."

"That would only make it harder for the nurses to care for them. These types of incidents don't happen often."

A callous remark to make. Even Jett knew the right answer. Once should be considered too much. "Will she recover?"

"She'll be fine," Chimera said, not evening looking his way. He placed a stethoscope on her chest for a listen. "Kyle. She's still struggling for air. Intubate her. Give her a thick oxygen mix. Increase the hemato drip"—which was for bruising and other flesh injuries—"and add a sedative. I want her to sleep through most of the repair."

Inwardly, Jett cringed as a breathing tube was rammed down her throat, but he couldn't deny her chest rose and fell more strongly and evenly after.

Chimera turned from the nurse, tucking his stethoscope in a pocket. "How is patient GL33?"

He shrugged. "Sleeping last time I saw him. Given he almost doubled in thickness when he was pissed, you're going to want to make sure you've got someone watching him even if restrained." Because it wouldn't be the first time the strength of a project surprised them and someone got hurt.

"He did seem rather strong, didn't he?" Chimera appeared pleased.

"Strong but dumb." He'd seen no sign of cognition or intelligence.

Chimera waved his concern away. "He just woke up. He'll need a few days to orient himself. You did good." In other words, good thing he'd not killed Chimera's project.

In the doctor's world, there were no failures. Every single patient, no matter the outcome, was a story to be learned from.

"What do you want to tell the girl?"

"I haven't yet decided." Chimera indicated the door. "I'll think of something and handle her when she wakes. You should return to your duties."

Dismissed.

Which was fine. Jett wanted nothing to do with the nurse. Yet, that didn't stop him from casting one last glance at her as she lay still on the bed.

Forever changed and she didn't even know it.

CHAPTER SEVEN

Waking up, Becky blinked at the bright lights overhead then panicked as she realized something had been rammed into her mouth and down her throat.

The foreign object made her choke as her throat acted reflexively to reject it. She rolled to her side, hands clasping at the plastic tubing, pulling at it.

"Easy, Nurse Frederickson. Let me help you. We didn't expect you to wake so soon."

How many times had she said the same thing when a patient woke in a panic?

Gentle hands rolled her until she once more lay on her back and then proceeded to remove the elastics holding the intubation tube in place against her mouth. Her gag reflex activated as the plastic slid free, and she coughed once she was free of it. A hard wracking sound that brought sharp pain to her lungs and a throb to her neck.

"Here. Drink this." A glass was presented to her, the fluid a strangely electric blue.

She tried to speak but only managed a croak. "Wassit."

The doctor tending her understood. "Just a little something to ease your throat."

Sounded heavenly. She brought the glass to her lips and then whimpered at the pain of swallowing the warm potion, a pain that receded the more she drank. By the time she finished the glass, the agony was but a dull throb in the background.

"Thank you" still emerged as a hoarse garble of noise, "Tnku."

"You need to let your throat rest while the medicine takes effect. It will remove most of the swelling overnight. You should be able to speak again by morning."

"Pity. The quiet is nice." She recognized the mumbled complaint and turned her head to see Jett standing on the other side of her bed.

She might have mouthed a not very Becky-like *Fuck you.* She'd almost died, and he was complaining about her talking? Asshole. Then again, she couldn't hate him too much. He was the one who came to her rescue. She had a vague recollection of him carrying her, maybe even telling her not to die. Which was crazy. Because that would mean he cared and he'd made it clear he didn't. Heck, he didn't even like her.

Pity, because she kind of liked him. Even if he was a jerk most of the time.

Damn him for being sexy and brooding. Why did he have to be the one who'd saved her?

The head of the bed lifted with a whir and sudden jolt of motion, the electronics moving it upward until she was seated. There was a doctor present—the white coat gave it away—one she'd not yet met, and Jett, who met her gaze with an undecipherable expression.

"You gave us quite the scare, Nurse Frederickson," the doctor said.

"Becky," she whispered.

"Becky." The man nodded. "And I'm Dr. Chimera."

The Dr. Chimera. Hot damn. She'd begun to wonder if he existed. She'd heard his name mentioned, but this was her first glimpse. She looked him over and felt a moment's surprise at his young age. Somewhere in his thirties, forties at the most. A tall guy, not quite as tall as Jett, with dark hair and vivid blue eyes.

He smiled, a comforting expression as he said, "Now, I know your throat is hurting, so I'm going to do most of the talking. You can nod for yes or shake for no. I promise this won't take long."

What wouldn't take long?

"When did the cancer return to your lungs?"

She blinked. How did he know? Only she and her oncologist knew the tumors were back, and too virulent to treat. She'd opted to forgo chemo, choosing to instead live out the rest of her days, however many those might be, on her terms.

"I can see by your expression that you knew about it. Knew even when you took this job."

She cringed. "Sorry."

"No talking, I said." He shook a finger at her, chiding. "And no need to apologize. Mr. Lowry was aware when he hired you of your medical condition. That MRI must have been a shock."

She mouthed *how*. Her records should have been sealed.

Chimera read her lips. "I have my ways. Needless to say, your lungs aren't looking good, Becky. I took some x-rays to evaluate the damage to your neck. Then I took some of your lungs. They're riddled with tumors."

"She's dying?" She heard the surprise in Jett's voice but didn't look at him.

She nodded. Her doctor had said she could have as much as a year left in her, or as little as six weeks.

Being the optimist sort, she kept hoping for a miracle.

"It is a death sentence," Chimera said bluntly. "And the worst part is I have something to help her." His eyes met hers. "The only problem is it is still in the experimental stages."

Her lips parted. He had a cure?

"The government," Chimera said the word with disdain, "they have all these rules about how we can test the drugs. At this point, we're still years away from human trials and yet"—he leaned close —"it works."

"You've used it?" she whispered.

Chimera winked. "That would be unethical of me. A shame, though, that someone like you has to suffer when the cure might be as simple as a few doses of this." He moved away to a refrigeration unit, opened it, and pulled out a vial. The fluid within shimmered, catching the light, iridescent in color, one moment blue, the next green, even silver. "This, my dear Becky, is the hope of the future. Clinical trials have shown it to effectively remove all signs of cancer in the lungs. As a matter of fact, the rats we've tested it on developed better lung capacity."

She held out her hand, and she didn't need to speak for him to understand her demand.

"I wish I could give it to you, Becky." Chimera

sighed. "But the rules..." He shook his head. "They say I can't."

As if she cared. It wasn't the journalist in her that wanted the cure but the scared, dying woman.

"Please."

"So sorry, but I can't. I already stepped over the line when using the osseous compound on you. But how could I not when you would have died without it?"

Her hand went to her throat. Her sore throat. Crushed. She'd seen one case during her tenure as a nurse. The patient wore a neck brace for life and had a trach tube to breathe.

Yet, she lived. Talked. All because he'd treated her, and now he thought she'd quibble over more experimental drugs.

"I'm dying."

"I know. Lucky for you, I had some leftovers of the compound. You wouldn't believe the demand for it by the various governments around the world. You've not got a million-dollar neck."

And garbage lungs.

"More?" she whispered.

"I wish I could, Becky. However, while the osseous compound is actually approved for clinical trials, the cancer drug isn't."

She wanted to sob as he turned from her and

placed it back in the fridge.

When he returned, he gave her a pitying look. "Let me talk to my contact in the government. Perhaps there's a way I can stress the importance of your situation and your willingness to try."

She nodded, a little too vigorously. The pain shot through her, and she gasped.

"How bad of me to keep you here talking when you should be resting. Jett. Escort nurse Frederickson to her room. Oh, but before you go..." Dr. Chimera turned his gaze on her. "Given your interest in my cancer research, I wonder if perhaps you'd mind transferring your services to another department. I find myself in need of an assistant. It would seem Kyle, my former aid, has fallen ill. It wouldn't involve any patients, per se. You'd be assisting me in my lab. That is, if you're interested?"

Work with the mysterious owner of the clinic itself? See exactly what he was doing? Maybe talk him into forgetting a few laws... Which was wrong. So wrong. And yet, a dying woman couldn't help having hope.

She managed to say, "Yes."

Dr. Chimera beamed and clasped his hands with a loud smack. "Then it's settled. In a few days, when you feel well enough, you'll begin working for me. Jett will show you how to get to my lab."

"Thank you."

"My pleasure. Now go rest. I'll have a special drink with some healing properties sent to your room after dinner. Be sure to drink it all up. And keep it secret," Chimera said with a wink. "Can't have everyone with a scratch or bruise begging for it. But it's the least I can do for you."

Chimera left, disappearing through a door with a flap of white coattails, leaving her alone with Jett. What a surprise, his face wore a scowl.

"Let's go." He jerked his thumb towards another exit. His bedside manner completely lacking.

He turned away, and she stuck her tongue out at his back.

Sliding her legs over the edge of the bed, she pushed herself to a standing position, only to feel her knees buckle and her head go light.

She almost hit the floor. Hands grabbed her before she planted.

Jett grumbled, "Jeezus fucking Christ, Red. Gonna make me carry you again?"

A part of her was tempted to glare at him. How dare he complain about the fact she still recovered from her injury? But her aunt always did say you got further with a smile and an unbuttoned blouse. She didn't have time to slip a few loops, but she could give him a winsome grin and a flutter of her lashes with a soft-spoken, "Please."

She held out her arms, and he sighed. "Ah for fuck's sake." He tugged her into his arms, the burly strength in them lifting her with ease.

She looped her hands around his neck and leaned her head on his shoulder, bringing her close enough to his neck that she smelled his aftershave. Something sharp and spicy. Very manly.

Sexy...

His long strides took them quickly down a long hall, and to her surprise, they emerged in the unfinished section of the tunnel on the habitat level.

A quick peek over his shoulder showed unblemished rock at his back.

"How?" she croaked.

"Camouflage. Now shut it. Doctor said no talking."

His rebuke clamped her lips tight. His grumbling annoyed. How dare he act so pissy. She'd almost died. It wasn't as if she'd asked for this to happen.

When he set her on her feet in her room, she wobbled. He kept his hands on her, steadying her, which was all she needed to get up on tiptoe and press her mouth to his.

She meant to kiss him as punishment. What she didn't expect was to enjoy it.

CHAPTER EIGHT

For a moment Jett stood frozen in place. She was kissing him.

Why the fuck did she have her mouth plastered to his?

Why wasn't he stopping it?

The woman had almost died. She was wounded, practically unable to speak, and yet her mouth had no problem latching onto his lower lip and making him feel things.... Things he shouldn't, below the belt.

Despite the arousal coursing through his body, he set her away from him. "Bad nurse," he admonished.

The rebuke brought a smile to her lips and a mischievous twinkle to her eyes. Much better than the pain of before.

"Feels good," she murmured.

Yeah, it had. Didn't make it right. "Don't do it again."

"Afraid your girlfriend will find out?" she taunted.

"I don't have a girlfriend." Realizing a moment too late she'd tricked him.

Her smile proved bright. "I'm single too."

He already knew that. Not that he was interested. No dating women at work. Or kissing.

"Get some rest," was his gruff reply. As opposed to his body, which thought he should drag her back into his arms for a more thorough kiss.

"Not tired," she croaked. "How Larry?" She kept her sentences short and clipped.

"Who the fuck is Larry?"

She gave him a pointed look, indicated her throat, then mimed choking herself and stuck out her tongue. It was horrifying and funny all at once. How could she be making fun of what happened already? Why did it tug a grin from his lips?

"The patient was taken to level six."

She cocked her head and waved her hand, indicating more.

"There is no more to tell. He woke up. He tried to pop your head off your shoulders. We tranqed his ass and took him to the basement." What he and the others called the more secure level for the violent ones.

Her lips pursed.

"Don't give me that look. What else did you expect?"

"He was disoriented. I am sure he didn't mean to hurt me," she said in a low, husky murmur.

"Don't make excuses for the asshole. He fucked up. As did you because you didn't listen to orders." The stink eye went well with his barked rebuke. "Next time, when you see one of the coma patients waking up, get the fuck out."

He blinked because, while her lips smiled and her eyes twinkled, the middle finger she raised proved eloquent.

And unexpected.

He laughed. "Oh, Red, I've seen and heard a lot worse than that."

"Tough guy." Said as an insult and paired with her taking a step closer.

He took one back.

The corners of her eyes crinkled.

The damned woman fucked with him. For the first time in his life, he didn't know what to do.

Can't kill her.

Couldn't even beat her.

Cursing her out was for bullies.

Which left only two options.

Kiss her or flee.

He swore he felt her mirth burning between his shoulder blades as he fled.

How dare she taunt him? He'd saved her sorry ass. If not for him, she'd be feeding the projects, part of a stew for the more carnivorous among them. The clinic didn't believe in wasting anything, not even human meat.

Why did she have to go and kiss him? Now the feel of her was imprinted on his mouth. His dick had ideas about what those lips would be good for. Hell, he had all kinds of ideas that involved her mouth, his cock, and naked skin.

Not happening.

The woman was a pain in his ass. She was dying. Broken.

Which bothered him. How could someone her age be so sick? She didn't look sick. However, he'd seen cancer before. Saw it take a man he once admired and reduce him to a shell. At one point, death was a mercy, and Jett didn't shed a tear when he helped his old friend to take that final step.

Since Chimera hadn't given him marching orders, Jett found himself heading for level six. It wasn't hard to figure out where they'd taken the newest patient. He could hear the bellowing down the hall, which explained the numerous guards who stood outside the door, guns aimed.

The sudden quiet eased the tension in the air only for a moment. There was a flurry of motion as the door opened, nervous fingers sitting on triggers.

A man in a white coat exited. "He's asleep," Doctor Cerberus announced, his voice rich with a hint of an accent. His dark skin contrasted with his jacket, and his graying hair appeared darker than the last time Jett saw him. "Keep two guards at the end of the hall. I want someone monitoring him twenty-four-seven."

"Yes, sir." Travis, one of the newer fellows recently expelled from the military and snagged by the clinic, practically saluted before he headed up the hall, the other guards at his heels. Jett gave them a nod as they passed and then went to meet with Cerberus.

The doctor had a tablet and was sliding his finger across it.

"Did they double his restraints?" Jett asked as he neared.

"We put him in the new titanium ones. He's a strong one."

"No shit. He almost killed the nurse that was with him when he woke."

"I heard. Might have been a blessing."

"What's that supposed to mean?"

The doctor tucked his tablet into a large pocket. "It means, given how sick that girl will become, the agony she'll go through, that a quick death might have been better."

"You know about her cancer?"

"I do."

"And you know Chimera has a cure for it."

"No, he has a prototype, unproven yet with humans."

Jett exploded. "Bullshit. You and I both know he's used it. Why not give it to the girl? It's not like he gives a shit about laws."

"No. He doesn't." Cerberus offered a faint smile. "However, he is picky about his patients, so there must be something about this woman that doesn't make her a viable subject."

"She's not military." Or ex-military. For some reason Chimera went after those who'd served. Which made no sense to Jett.

"He's made exceptions in the past for civilians. So there must be another reason."

"I don't give a fuck about his reasons. He's gonna let her die. Hell, he even taunted her with it. Showed her the cure then told her she couldn't have it."

Cerberus arched a brow. "How unusual. Almost as if he wants her to take it on her own."

A snort escaped Jett. "And how is that supposed to happen? He keeps the shit under lock and key."

"If Chimera wants her to have it, he'll find a way."

And if Chimera didn't, did Jett care enough to do it himself?

A few days ago, he would have said fuck her.

But she'd gone and kissed him. Now...now he didn't know what to think.

"What you gonna do with him?" He jerked his head at the door.

"The same as always. Study him. See what changes were wrought in his genes. Then tweak the formula for the next one."

Always experimenting, and yet Jett hadn't quite figured out their end goal. Some were easy to grasp. The cure for cancer would make the scientists and the clinic rich. But the other stuff—the stuff that made patients into something *else,* something more monster than man—he had no idea.

Chimera and his bevy of doctors like Cerberus and Sphinx kept playing with their mixtures, after something more than just healing.

Jett's best guess was they were looking to make super soldiers. The kind that could fight without weapons. Last longer. Be stronger.

Problem was, apart from a small handful, most of

the experiments were mindless shits. A soldier was no good if it turned on its own command.

"I hear the snipers spotted movement in the woods again," Jett remarked.

Awhile back, a foolish employee, feeling sorry for some of the patients, had made the grave mistake of setting them free. That employee was the first to die. And while some of those escapees had been caught, a larger number remained at large. Thought to be long gone or dead.

Until recently.

"We are aware of the increased activity and taking measures."

"Capture or kill?" Jett asked. Because, if the latter, he'd be miffed if no one called upon him.

"Neither. We've chosen observation for the moment. There must be a reason why they're watching."

Yeah. Revenge. But Jett held his tongue. "When is your kid coming to visit?"

"Jayda?" Cerberus beamed. "Next month. Which means we'll have to warn everyone." Because Jayda would be one of the few people allowed to visit and then leave. *If* she didn't see anything she shouldn't.

"We should take care of the problem in the woods before then," Jett suggested. Given his recent temperament, he could use something to calm him down. Hunting would fit the bill.

"We'll see. For the moment, we're going to watch. Maybe learn a few things. But fear not, when the time comes, we will request your services."

That time couldn't come soon enough. Especially since he found himself watching Becky that night. Watching and wondering what might have happened had he stayed.

CHAPTER NINE

Becky would have laughed as Jett fled if she didn't fear it would hurt. The man took off as if she would chase him. He'd enjoyed the kiss, even if he wouldn't admit it. The boner in his pants gave him away. What she didn't understand was why he ran away. Did a kiss scare him so much?

A thing to explore further if she didn't have more important things to ponder than his fear of making out.

She raised fingers to her throat, the ache in it demanding she find some acetaminophen or some other pain reliever. Entering the bathroom, she immediately glanced at the mirror and gasped at her reflection.

Her throat was a mottled, bruised mess. The

flesh puffy. Purple. Blue. Almost black in spots. Red in others.

Yet not crushed. Which was strange because, as she lay under Larry, his fingers digging, she could have sworn she heard something pop and crack. However, Dr. Chimera never even put her in a brace. Just implied he'd given her some top-secret treatment. But what kind of treatment healed crushed and broken bone?

Perhaps my injuries weren't as bad as I thought. She had, after all, passed out.

Leaning forward, she traced the damage and shuddered as she realized how close she'd come to dying. If Jett hadn't come to her rescue...

She'd have died a few months earlier than predicted and skipped the inevitable descent into pain.

A sigh escaped her. So much for hiding her diagnosis. Her boss knew the cancer was back, and then the jerk taunted her with the possibility of a cure. A cure she couldn't have because of the rules.

Which was ironic considering part of the reason she'd come here was in the hope of uncovering a scandal. She'd expected to find unethical medical practices. So far, though, she had nothing. Just a hint of the possibility of a cure, out of reach... Or was it?

Dr. Chimera had asked her to come work for

him. In his lab. This was her chance to not only finally get a grasp on what happened deep within the clinic but maybe, just maybe, convince the doctor to give her a taste of the cure.

Despite telling Jett she wasn't tired, it didn't take long to realize she needed sleep. She prepped for bed and had just about climbed into her sheets when there was a knock.

Probably Margaret. As it turned out, no one stood outside, but a tray had been left with a thermos. Opening it, she expected a vile concoction; however the fluid within, which steamed, had a smell similar to vanilla and, while it had a bit of a bitter undertone, went down smoothly.

It also put her right to sleep.

The next morning Becky woke with a sore head and an even sorer neck; however her smile had returned. Life was too short to be upset or grumpy. She knew this better than most.

And she also had another reason to grin. She'd kissed sourpuss Jett. Not that it would happen again. He knew her deadly secret. No man in his right mind would want to get involved with a dying woman.

It was part of the reason why she flirted and didn't follow through. It didn't seem fair to burden anyone. Which meant she spent more time alone than she enjoyed. It was also why she usually kept her door open and invited random people in. Not that many took her up on the offer. Only Margaret, as stuck up as she was, ever popped in to see her.

This morning, though, Becky didn't feel like opening the door. Not when she had secrets to write down. She'd not written much in her journal after her arrival. Mostly first impressions, a few wild speculations. Until Larry, the most excitement she'd seen was when they'd arrived and a patient on level six went a little nuts.

Since then? Nothing. While the clinic had a strange mode of operation, she'd not come across any illegal activity. Truly disappointing.

But she had a feeling she'd barely scratched the surface. Take for instance Dr. Chimera's secret lab. Why did the man keep it hidden?

And what of the concoction he'd given her? He implied he sold it to the military. Was it some kind of miracle cure being kept from the general public?

She tucked the journal under her arm and entered the bathroom. Gazing upon her reflection, she couldn't believe the difference from the night before. Craning her head, she noted most of the pain was gone, the bruising and swelling not as pronounced.

One would almost call her recovery miraculous. Sitting on her bed, with her legs tucked under her, she scribbled, detailing everything she remembered from the attack to Chimera's lab. Breaking who knew how many rules in doing so. She didn't care. What was the worst they could do to her?

They could send me away. Send her off to die alone instead of keeping her here where a cure might be hiding.

A knock at the door froze her. She tucked her journal inside her pillowcase. Not the greatest hiding spot, but then again, it wasn't as if this were a prison with guard searches on cells.

"Becky?" said Margaret from the hall, tapping again.

"Go away," she croaked, the hoarseness better than before but not completely gone.

"Are you okay?"

No. Far from it. But chances were, by now, word had travelled about the attack, which meant she couldn't exactly pretend it hadn't happened. "Fine. Just healing."

"Healing from what?" was Margaret's startled query.

The fact she'd not heard surprised Becky. Then again, the only two people who knew about the incident with Larry probably didn't talk about it. Becky was the one who'd slipped up, and Margaret seemed determined to see her.

Didn't it just figure. Becky sighed. A month she'd been trying to cultivate a friendship, and now that Margaret showed an interest, she just wanted her to go away. Best deal with this now. Becky opened the door just enough to peek out and say, "I had a problem with a patient. It's all cool now."

"What kind of problem?" Margaret shoved at the door, and Becky initially resisted, not wanting to deal with the censure she was sure Margaret would toss her way.

The other nurse walked in and gasped. "Your poor face. What happened?"

"One of the coma patients woke up. He was a little erratic." Understatement. He tried to kill her.

"A little?" was Margaret's incredulous reply. "He beat the hell out of you."

"Not his fault. He had no idea who I was. I'll be okay." Only because Jett had saved her and Dr. Chimera had given her some miracle potion. She knew better than to mention that part aloud.

"I'm so sorry."

"Don't be sorry. This is a good thing. Dr. Chimera gave me a promotion. Said I was wasting my time on the wards. I start in his secret lab tomorrow as his personal assistant." An unexpected boon. And one she was eager for. Finally, she might understand what was going on here—and maybe find a way to steal a taste of what he hid in his fridge.

"That sounds amazing." Margaret's reply was wooden.

It might be petty, but she kind of enjoyed the other woman's obvious jealousy. "It is." She couldn't help a faint smile.

Margaret glanced at her watch. "Shoot I have to run. My shift is about to start."

"Have fun." Becky waved and then shut the door. Leaned on it.

Weird how she was usually the one with her door open, encouraging Margaret and anyone else to visit. But today... Today she felt different.

For one, she had no interest in seeing or talking to anyone. People would ask questions she didn't feel like answering. She also wanted to process some of her memories. Memories of inhuman eyes that glowed. Just like the guy in the ER.

Whatever the cause, Chimaeram was obviously the source. Since she'd gotten special treatment, would her eyes glow, too? She ran to the bathroom to check. The same green orbs stared back. Perhaps she needed to be angry. Emotion seemed to trigger it.

Clenching her fists, she tried to irritate herself. Thinking of things that made her mad. Like no more pudding because she didn't eat fast enough. Or rain on a day she wanted fresh air. None of it was enough.

Her eyes remained the same.

Then again, what did she expect? It wasn't as if she'd been in a coma and given the IV like the other patients.

A knock at the door drew her attention. Probably Margaret again. Maybe with food. She was getting kind of hungry.

She opened her door, only to gape, as Jett stood in its frame. A flutter of pleasure erupted within, even as she reminded herself he'd probably not returned to claim another kiss.

"What are you doing here?" For a moment, she wondered if he'd come to give her the bum-rush out of here. A dying woman would be considered a liability no matter what Chimera or anyone said. She couldn't fault them for firing her.

Or maybe they knew about her journal and her plan to expose their secrets—once she found them—to the world.

Or—

"You look better," he stated.

Not exactly a glowing compliment. Heat still filled her cheeks. "I feel better. But how are you here? I thought this wing was for women only." Mr.

Lowry had showed Becky and Margaret when they first arrived what happened to men who strayed down the wrong hall. A giant zap that put them on the floor drooling.

"Exceptions can be made."

"Why are you here?" Had he come to check on her? The very idea warmed.

Then chilled as he said, "Chimera sent this." He thrust a thermos at her.

"What's in it?" she asked, taking it from him.

"Shit to make you feel better."

"Duh." She rolled her eyes. "I'm surprised you brought it. I didn't know you were his errand boy." Yeah, it was a dig; however, his attitude irritated. So much for that half-second when she thought he actually cared.

"I offered."

"You did?" The surprise lilted her reply.

He shifted uncomfortably, not meeting her gaze. "You were in rough shape."

"And you worried about me?" Would wonders never cease? "I'll be okay."

"No, you won't." Said bluntly.

"Because I'm dying." She shrugged. "We all have to die at one point."

"But you're young."

"Yup." How nice of him to point that out. She turned on her heel and moved away from the door.

"Doesn't it bother you?"

She whirled, eyes blazing. "Yes, it bothers me, but what should I do? Huddle in a corner and cry?"

"Why aren't you in a hospital fighting it?"

"Because I'm what you call terminal."

"You don't look sick."

"It will come. The cancer is spreading. Breathing hurts." A twinge with each lungful she took.

"Surely there's something you can do."

"No." She shook her head. "And you can stop pretending you care. We both know you don't. You're just freaked out by the fact I'm young and dying and cool about it."

"Bullshit."

"Excuse me?" She blinked at his profanity.

"I don't believe for a moment you're cool about it. I think you're pissed and scared and determined to not show it because if you show it then you have to face it."

"I'm already facing it. I've been facing the fact I'm going to die young for years."

"Then why aren't you fighting it?" he snapped back.

"Because I can't."

"Because you're afraid."

A sneer pulled her lips. "Do you really think you know me so well? The man who doesn't smile psychoanalyzing me. That's priceless."

"You saying I'm dumb?"

"I'm saying you wouldn't know emotions if they smacked you in the face."

At that, his lips curved into a smile. A slow, deadly, sexy smile that did things between her legs that made her wish he'd leave so she could have fun in her shower.

"I feel things, sweetheart. I'm just not some pansy-assed pussy who talks about them."

"Says the guy talking about them right now."

"I will deny it if asked."

"You assume I'd tell anyone. You're not exactly my main topic of conversation."

"I better not be. My business is my own."

"Yet you're involving yourself in mine?" she said with the arch of a brow.

"Yeah, well, someone has to because you apparently have a death wish."

"I don't want to die."

"So you claim, and yet I've twice had to save your ass."

"Twice?" It took her a second before she clued in and breathed, "It was you in the hospital who rescued me." It explained his familiarity.

"Wondering now if I should have bothered."

"I am not suicidal."

"Then fight." The last words he said before turning on his heel and leaving, meaning he missed her whispered, "But I don't know how."

CHAPTER TEN

WHAT THE FUCK POSSESSED HIM TO GO SEE HER? Even worse, Jett blathered like the biggest of pussies about caring.

Hello. He didn't fucking care. He'd made a career out of not caring.

At all.

About anyone.

Especially not a little bit of a woman with attitude who was dying. Surely there was a mistake in there somewhere.

However, Chimera had confirmed it not even an hour ago when he handed Jett the thermos.

"I heard you were talking to Cerberus about the nurse." A reminder that Cerberus, no matter how affable, owed his allegiance to one person.

"I was curious," Jett had replied, hedging.

"You were looking for a second opinion. But there's only one prognosis in this case. She's terminal."

As in no fucking hope—if she were anywhere else. "I've seen you cure cancer." Jett spoke boldly.

"I have. But you and I both know those I've saved are special cases." As in soldiers who, in the service of their country, agreed to become lab rats. The nurse, however, fell into the civilian category. They were a little harder to control, even with iron-clad contracts.

"So you don't tell her you're doing it." He shook the thermos. "Just like you didn't tell her what's in this."

"That formula has been patented and bought by the American government. It's legal. But my other cures..."

The other cures in this place weren't always a boon. Some had side effects. Terrible side effects. It was why Jett said no when he was offered a chance to try some of the lighter doses.

"She's dying. I'm sure she'd prefer a chance over nothing."

"I'm sure she would, too, but it won't be because I'm handing it to her."

"Then why tease her?" Jett couldn't get out of his mind that vial of fluid. The one Chimera dangled, taunting the nurse with it. Would Chimera be considered culpable if the woman happened to treat herself?

Jett had to wonder if that was the end plan given the doctor invited her to act as his personal assistant. Despite the fact there was nothing wrong with Kyle.

None of his business. Just like those kept beyond Chimera's lab in those cages were none of his business. In every venture there would be failures.

His job was to track them if they escaped.

Speaking of, the night crew had nabbed yet another of the missing patients. For some reason, they'd begun to return, hiding in the nearby forest. Watching. Always watching.

For what? He kind of wanted to find out. Because, by his count, there were at least a half-dozen or so still at large. Maybe more if Chimera neglected to tell him of other escapees.

Why did they linger nearby? Why now after all this time?

Was it any wonder he asked for a real handgun and not this tranquilizer bullshit? The reply? *"No. I want them brought in alive."* Never mind those who died in the attempt. Their lives weren't as valuable as Chimera's pet projects.

After dropping off the thermos—clenching his fists to avoid the temptation Becky posed with her full, pouty lips and tousled hair—he went to visit the secret room beyond Chimera's lab. Firstly, because Chimera ordered him to, and secondly, because he had to see for himself. See the thing in the cage, a monster instead of the man he once knew.

Yes, monster, and Jett knew about them. One of the few in this place aware of the secrets—and failures. Not all guards had a free pass to go anywhere they liked. Jett had proven himself loyal. Proven he'd do anything to keep company secrets.

Anything but take the various remedies himself. He had no interest in being more than human. Then again, he'd not suffered like some of those who'd agreed.

People like Jorge, a man he'd met during his own basic training.

Left for dead on the battlefield, the same gunfight that also damaged Chimera's star patient, Luke, Jorge had only two options: Die because his wounds were so grievous or say yes to a chance. A chance to not only live but become more than he was.

While Luke was an example of what a man could become—stronger, faster, and more dangerous than any loaded weapon—Jorge became the poster child for side effects. And those unfortunate quirks kept multiplying.

Jorge should have run when he had the chance. He was one of those who'd escaped. Then foolishly returned.

Had he missed the safety of his cage?

Jett entered the lab, ignoring the various beakers and vials, the steady hum of the machinery familiar. He strode past it all—even the fridge with that taunting serum that could save a certain nurse—right to a door that yielded to his palm print. He entered that secret room, full of cages, only one of them occupied.

The first sight of Jorge brought a low whistle.

"Well. Well. I always knew you were a pig, but this..." Jett shook his head. "Damn."

A baleful glare met his. The man, once a thick Mediterranean fellow with olive skin and dark hair, now something else. The last time Jett had seen him was a few months ago before his escape. His appearance had changed since then.

"Better a pig than a boot licker," was the gruff reply. The words thick as they emerged from a mouth no longer human shaped. The jaw was elongated, and the nose had flattened. The tusks provided an interesting accessory jutting from either cheek.

"It's not boot licking but following orders. Orders that pay me very well."

"You're a traitor."

Jett uttered a low chuckle. "I'm the traitor? I seem to remember someone turning tail and running rather than sticking by his brothers." It was why Jett had shot Jorge in the leg during a military operation. He had no use for cowards.

"You're a fucking psycho."

"Thank you." The compliment earned Jorge a smile. "Now that we've gotten the pleasantries out of the way, why are you here?"

"Because some assholes put me in a cage." The exclamation finished on a growl.

"Those assholes, as you call them, wouldn't have caught you if you'd kept on hiding in the mountains. Yet you returned. Why?"

A sneer pulled part of Jorge's snout. "Why do you think? Revenge."

"Revenge for what? You agreed to this." Jett swept a hand to encompass the room around them.

"I agreed because I was scared, and I thought I had no other choice." The shattered spine and the organs failing hadn't left much of an option.

"You had no other choice. It's only because of this clinic you're alive. They gave you a second chance," Jett remarked. "Their treatment is why you're even walking again."

"He made me into a monster!" Jorge grabbed the

bars, the hiss of sizzling flesh lasting a moment before he tore them free.

"A monster because you ran away before he could fix you." Not the entire truth. Chimera didn't care about the man, only the result.

"Damned right I ran. And I'll escape again. And again, until I tell the fucking world what he's doing here. What you are all doing. You'll pay." Spittle flew as Jorge got riled.

"Bullshit." Jett leaned closer. "You escaped. You could have done that. But you didn't. You came back. Why?"

Eyes glowing with malice fixed Jett. "Because I'm hungry. So very, very hungry... And there's only one thing I want to eat." The man/beast slammed into the bars over and over, shoving his arm through, reaching for Jett.

He stood out of reach, doing his best not to react to the singeing flesh. He brought his walkie-talkie to his lips and pressed the button. "He's gone feral."

The channel only went to one person. It took a moment before Chimera replied. "We need some fresh samples. Put him on ice."

Jorge had just run out of second chances.

Jett shook his head as he neared the flailing arms. "You should have kept running." He whipped out a baton and slammed it on a protruding wrist. Jorge screamed, more rage than pain. Jett deactivated the current running through the bars and stepped even closer.

Jorge stood just out of reach and glared balefully at him. "You're as evil as them."

"Yes." Jett had no doubt of his guilt. But if Jorge thought to invoke pity or remorse, then he'd obviously not read the psychiatric reports.

Jett reached through the bars, only to have Jorge back out of reach.

"Are you really going to make this difficult?"

"I don't want to die," Jorge whimpered. The big, strong monster gone, in his place a man who realized he might have fucked up.

"Then you should have thought of that before you came back." Jett unlatched the cage door and let it swing open. He held himself braced in case Jorge tried to rush him.

"Don't do this. Let me go. Please." Jorge dropped to his knees, head bowed.

Begging. How pathetic. And yet...a tiny part of him hesitated. The man hadn't asked to become this thing. Not asked to be put in a cage.

Jorge dove at him, slamming into Jett's thighs, throwing him into the bars of the cage. This wasn't his first rodeo. Jorge snapped and snarled, his teeth locking on flesh covered in fabric. A hard chomp that would leave a bruise.

Jett didn't need to use his teeth. The knife sliced across the other man's jugular. The arterial spray was an unfortunately messy side effect.

Jorge shoved away from Jett, putting a hand to his neck, trying to stem the arterial blood. But Jett had cut deep.

He stepped out of the cage and grabbed some paper towels to mop at the wetness coating him. He'd have to shower before he showed his face in the public areas. Behind him, he heard crashing and thumping. The dying throes of a coward.

Jett finished mopping his face and turned to look at the body lying on the floor. The eyes wide open and staring. He changed the channel on his walkie-talkie before barking, "Travis and Burke."

"Yeah?" was the reply.

"I've got a subject that needs to be iced, asap." The doctors hated it when bodies were left sitting and began to decay. They also preferred bodies that bled out rather than those drugged to death or killed with a bullet to the head. It made for more thorough autopsies. When a subject stopped being useful alive, they served in death.

Being the executioner didn't usually bother Jett, but as he watched them sluice down the cage, the red water swirling down the drain in the floor, he couldn't help but think of Red.

With cancer riddling her body, soon she, too, would stare with eyes wide open. A piece of meat for scientists to study.

And he didn't like the thought one single bit. But getting involved? Trying to save her?

He could do it. Break into that special vault of remedies. The thing was, would that end up being a cure or a curse?

CHAPTER ELEVEN

T WO DAYS AFTER THE INCIDENT, A PEEK IN THE mirror showed the bruises on her throat a sickly yellow. Better than expected, but still a stark reminder of what happened.

A knock at the door shattered the reverie. Opening the door revealed Jett, which wasn't entirely surprising given he'd dropped off another thermos last night. A visit that lasted all of two seconds with him shoving it at her, snapping a gruff, "Drink it." Then he took off.

So of course, she yodeled after him, "Run, run as fast as you can..." No point in finishing the rhyme. He was out of sight, her last view of him being the index finger raised over his shoulder.

Had to admit she didn't mind the rear view of him. Those combat pants hugged his ass in a mighty fine way. She'd have to make sure to picture it later in the shower. Without the scowl he currently sported.

He stood in the doorframe, hands empty, looking as surly as ever. "Why aren't you ready?" he barked.

She tucked a chunk of hair behind her ear and peeked down at her garb. A pajama set covered in cute, cuddly kitties. Pink ones of course. Poor Jett. It was the equivalent of a cross to a vampire.

"Good morning to you, too."

He glared.

Only one thing to do.

Smile.

"Do you always scowl this early in the morning?"

"You aren't dressed."

Her lips twitched. "Shouldn't an undressed woman in the morning be a reason not to scowl?"

"I always have a reason."

"Not this morning you don't." She whirled from the door. "You accused me of not being ready. Problem is you never told me to be ready or what time. So this is entirely your fault."

"My fault?" The incredulous note had her smiling as she stood facing away.

"It is, and you were mean about it. I won't have it." She whirled and crossed arms under her breasts. It had the effect of shoving them a little higher and farther out of her shirt. Wasn't her fault the nipples were hard. The blame for that also resided with him.

He didn't have to stare, but she enjoyed it. For a few seconds at least, then she said, "Eyes here." She snapped her fingers, and his shocked gaze met hers. His cheeks turned a shade darker, and she'd never seen anything sexier.

Especially when he mumbled, "Can't blame a guy for staring if you're going to be wearing practically nothing."

"I will blame him since he showed up at an ungodly hour. And not only did you not bring me coffee, you couldn't even fake a smile."

"Are you still harping on that?" He pulled his lips wide, showed a lot of teeth, and said in a low growl, "Is this better?"

"Put that thing away, it's frightening," Becky exclaimed.

"Never happy, are you? First, she complains I'm a humorless dick, and now my smile ain't good enough."

He harangued without real heat as he leaned against her doorframe. Casual as could be, and oh look, a bed not far from them.

She moved to her closet and pulled out some clean clothes, saying over her shoulder, "Oh I think you have a sense of humor. The kind that laughs when people fall off skateboards or electrocute themselves." She turned around to toss her garments on the bed and caught the genuine grin that finally graced his face.

No wonder he hid it. The man was bloody gorgeous when he used it. And he had a dimple.

1. Dimple.

A deadly combination.

"You forget to mention getting nailed in the balls."

"Is that what it would take to make you laugh? Hitting you in the sac?" She arched a brow.

"I wouldn't recommend trying it."

"Are you sure? My ball-handling skills are quite stellar." She turned away, lest he see her biting her lip to keep from laughing.

Since he didn't immediately reply, or seem inclined to leave, she grabbed the hem of her top and pulled it off. Only her bare back showed, and yet she felt exposed, utterly conscious of the fact he remained in the room.

Did he stare?

He did. "What are you doing?" Asked in a very low voice.

"You told me to get ready, remember?" She

finished snapping the hooks of her bra before turning around, doing her best to think bathing suit. The bra acted like a bikini top.

Except she'd never had a man's gaze smolder when she went somewhere to tan.

"I'll be in the hall. Come out when you're ready." He abruptly left.

Her giggles might have chased him. She quickly finished dressing and spent a moment freshening her hair and adding a bit of makeup.

When she exited into the hall, Jett leaned a few paces away, seemingly negligent, and yet, she saw how he stiffened the moment she stepped out.

"About time," he drawled.

"Given I'm sure it takes you longer to get that perfect 'I am the bringer of doom and gloom' look every morning, you can stop with the insults."

"Or what?"

"I have ways of making you beg for mercy." Her glance dropped south of his waist.

His hand slid down to cover the growing bulge. "Not interested, Red."

"Did someone forget to tell your little friend?" She played with fire. She knew it. Teasing and taunting, yet she couldn't help herself.

"Nothing little about it."

"Says you. I demand proof." She took a step closer to him.

Jett stood his ground despite the muscle jumping in his cheek. "It's not going to work."

"What isn't?" Slanting him a glance through partially shuttered lashes, she pursed her lips.

"Whatever it is you're doing."

"You're scared of me. And yet you shouldn't be. I won't be around long enough to matter."

Shock widened his eyes.

But she was done playing. The flirting only served to remind her what she couldn't have.

She stepped past him. "I take it you're here to conduct me to my new assignment."

"I'm supposed to escort you to Chimera's lab."

"Not as simple as walking through a solid-seeming rock wall?"

"It's simple once you know where to look. Follow me." That sexy strut took him up the hall. At the juncture, he halted and cast a glance back, impatience in his expression. Which was why she slowed her steps and smiled. "What's the weather like outside today? And more important, are they serving bacon for breakfast? Do you know they actually had the nerve to have sausage only last Tuesday morning? Me, eating sausage. Mind you, I don't mind a mouthful of thick meat but—"

As she caught up, he growled, "You're pushing it, Red."

"If you're nice, maybe I'll be tugging it, too." Said with a wink then a smothered giggle as he made a noise that screamed frustration. The dirty kind.

There was something fun about driving him a little nuts.

Turning into the hallway under construction, she looked back and saw someone going the other way. "Won't people wonder what we're doing down here?"

"They'll assume we're fucking," was his blunt reply.

"Well that's no good."

He cast a glance over at her. "Are you going to whine about your reputation?"

"No." She laughed. "More worried about yours. You don't seem like the type to take women in the halls."

"Is that so?" he drawled. "And just what type am I?"

She pretended to ponder it a moment before saying, in a husky low tone, "The kind who likes to lie on his back in bed and let a woman take control." Because how sexy would it be to have a man this big and strong underneath her, at her mercy?

"You got the bed part right. A man likes something soft for his knees when he's pounding from behind."

"Behind?" she repeated as he stopped at the dead-end rock wall. "I guess I shouldn't be surprised you're all about your own gratification."

"What's that supposed to mean?" He shot her a dark stare.

"Just that doggy style is more about the man's pleasure. If you're the kind of lover who likes his partner to come with him, then missionary or cowgirl is the way to go."

"Who says I don't take care of her first?" The sultry look melted every single bone in her body. She was ready to throw herself at him and say, *"Show me!"*

Why had he suddenly started flirting back? She could handle him when he was a jerk, but this teasing, sexy man?

"You think of someone else's pleasure first?" She snorted. "I highly doubt that. You've got selfish written all over you." She ignored him to stare at the rock. Touched it as well and felt the rough surface, solid and cold.

"You're touching the wrong spot." For a moment, when he tugged her hand, she thought he might put it on his crotch. Instead, he shoved it into the mirage wall. "This is where you scan your card."

"What on Earth?" She stared down at their arms, the wrists appearing severed at the rock. Yet she could feel the firm grasp of his fingers. The tingle that spread at his touch.

"Told you. Holograms." He pulled free and stepped to the side. "Activate it."

She retrieved her card and tried not to flinch as she shoved it into seemingly solid stone. She scraped the edge of her hand on rock. She was too far to the left, but she heard the click of locks disengaging nonetheless as her card came close enough to the reader to engage it.

Visually nothing had changed. She frowned. "So now what?"

"Now you enter."

"Enter where? There?" She pointed at the wall she'd touched. "That's rock. Real rock."

"Not all of it. The door opened under the notched piece."

"What if it didn't open? I'll smash my face."

"You can check first." He shoved his arm up to the shoulder through the wall. "See. Open."

"You go first."

"Don't be a pussy."

"I'm not a pussy. I want to see you use it first." Given the number of horror movies she'd watched, the first person through usually got devoured by the monster. She preferred not to dwell on what sometimes happened to those who stayed behind.

"We used this entrance the other day."

"Go. I'll follow." She shooed him.

"I am not getting paid enough for this." He sighed and disappeared from sight, passing through the rock, leaving her alone.

Kind of freaked her out. Excited her, too, because this was truly epic stuff. Hidden doors and holograms. What else would she encounter?

Feeling much like Alice must have the first time she went down the rabbit hole, she closed her eyes and stepped in.

CHAPTER TWELVE

JETT SNICKERED AS HE SAW RED STEP THROUGH, eyes shut tight. Her trepidation amused, which might be why he quickly stepped in front of her and held still as she rammed into him.

"Darn it!" Her arms flailed as she weaved on her feet.

He caught her before she could fall. "Watch where you're going, Red."

There was no glare in her gaze or censure when her eyes opened. Rather mirth. "Ha, ha, funny guy. You might be rock solid, but your shirt gave it away."

A man could only swell in pride at her comment. "Never walk into situations with your eyes closed."

"I'm a little too old and far-gone for lessons in life."

The reminder flattened his lips. As they went through the hall, he noticed her glancing around.

"Those aren't just air ducts, are they?" she said.

"Don't know what you're talking about."

"Look at them. They run the whole length of the hall."

"Part of the decontamination system. Don't move."

"Wh—Ack. Ugh." The misting spray hit her, and she grimaced.

He waited until it dissipated before saying, "Keep your mouth shut if you don't want your tongue disinfected."

"Next time a warning beforehand would be helpful."

"But that would ruin my entertainment." Jett winked before opening the door into the lab proper.

"There's my star patient and new assistant." Chimera sounded entirely too cheerful. Fake, too, considering less than twenty minutes ago Jett had caught him in a full-blown tantrum over some test results he didn't like.

"Good morning, Dr. Chimera. Sorry I'm late. Jett forgot to tell me what time I'd be starting."

"Not too late, especially considering I haven't gone to bed. Exciting things are happening, my dear."

Exciting if you counted the fact that two subjects up and died overnight, bleeding out of every orifice with no sign as to why.

"I can't wait to learn. Where do you want me to start?"

"I love your attitude. Jett, now that you've brought Nurse Frederickson to me, you can call it a night. Or is that a day?" The doctor chuckled at his own lame attempt at a joke.

Dismissed. Totally expected, and yet leaving her didn't sit right. For one, he didn't entirely trust Chimera. The man plotted something. He always plotted.

Still, Jett couldn't refuse a direct order.

He turned on his heel and tried not to wonder if he'd ever see her again.

He shouldn't have worried. Staying away from her didn't prove to be an option. Chimera had him reassigned. Put him to watching her on the cameras, ready to act at a moment's notice if needed. Not that he could figure out what he'd be protecting her from. She was only given access to the main lab. The only dangerous thing in there were her own two clumsy feet.

He hated the new job. Not only did he have to sit for hours at a time watching a boring screen, he had to watch *her*.

It proved a strange form of torture, especially because everything she did drew him, from the way the tip of her tongue stuck out when she concentrated to the roundness of her ass when she bent over. She didn't do it consciously, yet she tempted him.

Then to make matters worse, he couldn't help himself from running into her in person. If she went for breakfast, he soon followed. Outside for a walk, he suddenly had an urge for a rare cigarette.

In his defense, he followed orders. Dr. Chimera possessed a very suspicious mind. Despite all his security precautions, he remained convinced that she might betray.

Jett joked with the doctor, *"You think she's gonna write a message and tie it to a pigeon with connections to the outside world."*

Rather than laugh, Chimera eyed him quite seriously and said, *"Actually, foxes make for better carriers."*

So he spied on her to allay his boss's mind. Stalked her really. And the worst part? The thing that pissed him off the most?

He enjoyed it.

What he didn't enjoy as much was the inexplicable jealousy. Take the other evening for instance. She'd spent two hours in the communal area watching some movie that had her giggling. It drew attention. All of the young attractive women did, and so when she left, it was quite normal for the guys remaining to discuss her.

"I wouldn't mind tapping that," said Barry as he lined up his cue to hit a ball.

"Think she's into tag teaming?" Len threw the comment out just as Barry pulled back, totally skewering his shot.

"With those lips, she can probably suck a golf ball through a garden hose." Barry suctioned his cheeks.

"And she swallows," confided Abe with a shit-eating grin. Problem was Jett knew for a fact he lied.

"She's never touched you," Jett announced, his low timbre nonetheless carrying.

"What?" Abe absently said as he rubbed chalk on the end of his cue.

"I said she ain't ever touched you. So why you talking smack about her?"

This time Abe heard him and turned. The smirk on his face antagonized. "Who says she didn't?"

"I do."

"And I guess you'd know given how often the two of you end up going down Construction Alley together," Abe said with a sneer.

Odd how it didn't bother him that they thought

he slept with her. What bothered him was other assholes discussing it. "Take it back. Admit you lied."

"Or?" Abe, being a newer fellow, obviously hadn't been paying attention to the rumors. Jett knew there were plenty about him. All of them mentioned his temper.

Which flared.

"Or I am going to spank your ass in front of your buds until you snot and cry for mercy."

"You and what fucking army?" Abe stood tall, a big dude, probably at least twenty or thirty pounds heavier than Jett.

Didn't matter. Jett was born meaner. He advanced on the other guy while Travis, a good shit, if too stupid to know when to get out of the way, inserted himself. "Jett, he isn't worth it."

"He's lying."

"No, I'm not. That nurse Becky is a whore. A cock-sucking—"

Smack.

Jett punched him. Right in the face. Abe recoiled but didn't fall.

"Mother fucker." He charged at Jett, who treated him like a bull and swept aside at the last minute then snared the other man with a foot.

Abe went tumbling. Jett pounced, shoving his knee in the man's chest, an arm braced across his neck, and his mouth close enough to hiss, "You should have apologized."

"Fuck. You."

Jett smashed his head against Abe's nose and felt a moment of satisfaction at the sharp scream.

Only then did he rise. Glance coldly at those watching. "Anyone else want to disrespect the ladies in this place?"

Frantic head shakes all around.

"Good."

Abe, though, still hadn't learned his lesson. "I'm going to fucking report you." The words wet and bubbly as he bled copiously from the nose and mouth.

"Go ahead." Jett smiled. "I dare you."

And perhaps he did. Because the next time he saw Abe, the fucker mumbled, "Sorry."

But sorry wasn't enough. Chimera didn't tolerate trouble-makers, which was why Jett wasn't surprised when Abe ended up in a cage in the secret lab, strapped to a bed, asleep, with a bile-yellow IV stuck in his arm.

CHAPTER THIRTEEN

He was watching her again.

Funny how Jett always had an excuse every time she saw him. He just happened to suddenly be grabbing meals at the same time as her. Just happened to indulge in a game of billiards when she came to watch the newest movie for the residents.

Kind of flattering, except for the fact he never came near her. Pretended not to look at her. Avoided actual contact or speech. Yet, she was aware of him. Every single nerve ending tingled when he appeared.

Was it the same for him?

She had just about decided to tackle him in a hall and demand to know what his problem was when he appeared in the lab.

Tall, dark, and scowling. "Let's go."

Taking her time, peeling her gloves, she replied, "Go where? And if you're about to say your bedroom, then I should warn you I am wearing granny panties. But if cotton's your thing, then I'm good to go."

Ah, the sweet look of confusion on his face. "We're going outside."

"Outside to do what? This better not be the start to a slasher movie where you chase me through the woods."

He blinked at her. "Jeezus, Red, how the fuck does your mind work?"

"In weird and mysterious ways. And I wouldn't talk. Look at you." She deepened her voice. "Come. Now. Me. Say. So." She thumped her chest.

He didn't appear impressed with her caveman impression. "Chimera ordered me to take you outdoors for some fresh air. Apparently, it's been a few days since you've been out of the lab. So move your ass, or I will drag you."

"By the hair, Neanderthal style?" she teased, but she did remove her white overcoat. And thank God she no longer had to wear that stupid nursing cap

It surprised her Chimera had ordered her to get some fresh air. She wouldn't have expected the man to remember that a human body needed a glimpse of the sun. He worked her hard. She never had a moment to sit still. Drawing blood from the rats he kept in the far corner. Giving them coded serums, their colors reminding her of the time she spent working in the coma ward. She spun vials. Added drops. Prepared slides. Entered data. Given all her duties, she acted more scientist than nurse, and yet, the work proved fascinating.

Even if she didn't quite understand what he did, there existed a certain excitement in working closely with Chimera. The man's mind worked a mile a minute. Always thinking. Observing.

Was it his skills of observation that saw her staring overly long at Jett? Whatever the reason, the orders were for Jett to take her for a walk.

She almost asked him if he'd brought a leash.

Before leaving to go outside, she grabbed a sweater. The fall arrived earlier in the mountains, the crisp breezes holding a promise of the winter to come.

They made it outside without saying a word. A bit of a record for Becky. However, she wanted to see how long it took before he broke it first.

He waited until they got to the worn dirt track the inhabitants of the clinic used.

"How are you feeling?"

For once she didn't note any mockery, or disdain. A hint of concern? Possibly.

"Not bad actually." The tickle in her lungs remained. The occasional sharp stab. But nothing she couldn't handle. But just in case, she'd begun stockpiling pain meds, going to the doctor at the clinic who dealt with employee ailments. Claiming a migraine got her a handful of pills each time. She had quite the collection now.

"Hmmm." The grunt ended that line of talk.

Looking over at the woods, she remembered something she overheard in the cafeteria. "Is it true someone got attacked by a monster in the woods?"

"Hardly a monster."

"So what was it? Bear? Wolf? Mountain cat? Yeti?" She named a bunch of things.

His reply? "Yup."

"Yup, to what?"

"Does it really matter? The thing that attacked that nurse is dead. You don't have to worry about it."

"I'm not scared."

"Maybe you should be. There's danger in those woods. Remember that."

"I will." She stopped and stared at the dark pockets between the dense trees. It would be easy to get lost. As the temperature at night kept getting colder, the risk of death by exposure if a person remained outdoors increased. Add in wild animals and it meant she had a plan in mind for when the pain got too intense.

"Hey." He snapped fingers in front of her. "Don't you go thinking like that."

"I don't know what you mean."

"I served in the army. I know that look."

"And what look would that be?" she asked, shoving her hands into the pockets of her sweater.

"The one that says you wanna die but don't want to pull the trigger yourself."

She shrugged. "You caught me. Can you blame me? I know what's coming." The pain. The agony. The pleading with someone to end it.

"You're a nurse. Use some pills."

"Pills aren't a sure thing and not exactly plentiful around here." Being ensconced in a clinic meant not having access to any of the good stuff. The stash she'd managed would barely take off the edge.

"Then you ask for help if it gets too bad."

At that, she snorted. "Are you seriously telling me I should ask someone to kill me when the cancer gets to be too much?"

"Better than walking in the woods looking to get mauled by a bear."

"So it was a bear."

"Would you stop focusing on the fucking animal

we killed?" He grabbed her by the arms and frowned. "I am trying to be serious."

"Why?" She stared at his face, noticing his intent expression.

"Hell if I know why. You're the most annoying woman I've ever met."

"Yet here you are walking me around and giving me advice on offing myself." She pulled herself free. "Again, I have to ask, why?"

"Fucked if I know." He kicked the ground.

"I do. You pity me." The one emotion she couldn't handle. Was that all he saw when he looked at her? A sad and broken woman?

She swept past him only to feel herself yanked back as he snared her by the arm.

"Don't get all pissy. Yeah, I feel sorry for you. You're going to die. And that blows."

"It does. But I've come to terms with it. And so should you." Tears stung at her eyes.

"Ah, don't fucking cry."

"Don't tell me what to do."

She walked away from him, arms wrapped around herself. Hating him for prying open the shields she kept around her emotions. Didn't he understand what a tentative grip she had on sanity? No one wanted to die. No one wanted to deal with it.

Hearing a shout, she looked over her shoulder and saw someone walking toward Jett. Given he was busy, she wandered away from him toward the lake. Not her favorite thing in the world, if she were honest.

Something about the cold water brought a chill to her bones. Reminded her of the middle of the night when she woke in a sweat, a cold sweat, gasping for air.

Staring into the cold depths, she saw movement. Darting shapes. Their scales shimmering as they sluiced through the water. The deep, deep water. She'd heard say that the lake was considered almost bottomless given it went far below any of the sensors they'd used in an attempt to measure.

Why, a person could step off this very edge and sink so long and so far no one would ever find the body. Nor would a person survive. The temperature remained only a touch above freezing, the glacier melt from the mountains feeding the lake and keeping it chilly no matter how bright the sun shone.

The water had a translucent beauty to it and must have had a mirroring effect because, for a moment, she saw herself reflected in it. But her in a way she'd never imagined. Her hair floating in a sinuous halo around her face. Her skin pale. So very pale. The slender fingers of her hand reaching. The mouth opening to whisper, *Join us*.

It would be so quick. Easy. Painless.

The water version of herself beckoned, and she felt herself sway.

Then get yanked from the edge.

"What the fuck are you doing?" Jett barked. "If you fell in here, you'd sink like a rock."

"And?" She turned a tired gaze on him. "Don't pretend you care."

"I care more than I should."

"Bullshit." The expletive spilled from her. "We both know you don't give a damn."

"Don't presume to tell me what I think." He glared.

Her chin lifted a notch. "I think you're mistaking feelings with pity. And I don't need either. If you'll excuse me. I've had enough fresh air for today."

She swept past him, half hoping he'd grab her by the arm and tell her it wasn't pity he felt but...what? What did she want from him?

Love.

Which was a foolish wish. Not to mention a selfish one. Jett didn't love her. Nor did she want him to. Yet tell that to the empty spot inside her that yearned for someone to hold her tight.

Not just someone. Him. For some reason he was

the one who filled her thoughts, who made her feel safe. Which was dumb because he couldn't protect her from the one thing that would kill her.

With her mind in turmoil, she spent the night in her room, drinking hard. Hard enough that she passed out and slept through her alarm. By the time she realized what had happened, she was running late. Super late.

Despite that, she jumped into the shower. The hot water sluiced down her body, and she sighed. Her hands roamed over her skin, lingering more than they should. Times like these, when she was alone, she allowed herself to fantasize.

Imagined Jett in the shower with her, stroking his hands all over her naked and slick body.

Between her legs, her sex throbbed. Begging for the touch of her fingers. But as she stroked her slick folds, she pretended it was his mouth. A hot pair of lips, tugging and sucking. His tongue dipping.

Her breath caught. As one finger stroked between her nether lips, the other hand gripped her breast. Pinching her hard nipple. Rolling it and tugging, sending sweet jolts to her pussy.

Her finger dipped out of her sex to glide over her swollen clitoris. She rubbed it, faster and faster.

So close.

So...

"What are you doing?" The object of her fantasy gasped.

With a squeak, she pressed herself against the cold tile wall of her shower. The glass barrier that acted as a curtain did nothing to hide her. Two hands couldn't shield all her parts.

Jett wasn't the kind of guy to look away. His eyes half lidded, he drank her in, and she shivered. Arousal coursed through her still, even increased at her audience.

If she continued to masturbate while he watched, would he watch? Join in? Oh God.

"What are you doing here?" she asked instead of inviting him to get naked and on his knees.

"You didn't come in to work so I came to check on you."

"I slept in."

"Apparently. You could have let someone know."

"I didn't expect anyone to care."

"I care." His lips pressed tight as if he regretted the admission.

"Well I'm fine. Which you would have known if you'd knocked."

"I did knock. You didn't answer."

Probably because between the ventilation fan and the shower she'd not heard a thing. "You can't just barge in whenever you like."

"I will if I think there's reason." He stepped closer, his frame imposing in the small bathroom.

Sexy, too, if wearing too many clothes.

"What possible reason could you have for entering my room uninvited?"

"I was worried about you." The soft words hit her in the gut. Anything else, she might have had a reply.

But this...

"I'm fine, as you can see. Just tired."

"Me too."

"Not sleeping well?" she asked as he strayed even closer, close enough she could have reached out and touched him.

"You might say that. I've been having dreams lately." He slid the glass door to the side.

"Of what?" The words barely made it past her lips. Did he dream of waters that drowned too?

"You." A knuckle brushed down her cheek, and she turned into the touch, eyes closed, wondering if she slept still because surely he hadn't admitted to having thoughts of her.

"I told you not to worry about me."

"Can't help myself. I keep telling myself to stay away. To ignore you."

"But?" she asked on a breathless whisper.

"You're the one thing I can't stop thinking

about." His hand cupped her chin and dragged her closer.

"What are you doing?" She stared at him, her heart beating so hard it might actually escape her chest.

"Trying to quiet the demons."

What demons?

All thought fled as his mouth met hers, a softer embrace than she would have imagined despite his hard lips. He kissed her slowly, languorously as the shower at her back steamed the room.

She found herself sitting on the counter, ass on the cold marble top, his body pressing between her thighs as he kissed her still, his fingers twined in her hair.

A pat of her wondered at his change of heart, and another part thought she should stop, but the strongest part of her reveled in his caresses. Had craved this from almost the moment they met.

With Jett, she felt alive. She felt desire.

Even a silly ounce of hope.

She peeled the shirt from his upper body. He had a rock-hard physique, the top of him broad and muscled. The planes smooth and yet ridged. Her mouth followed her hands, tasting skin, while his hands gripped her hips.

When he suddenly dropped down, she made a

sound, disappointed at losing her new playground. Only to gasp as he parted her thighs and blew on her.

Was this really happening?"

The first lash of his tongue against her clit let her know it was. She grabbed him by the hair and writhed at his touch. Keened at the pleasure. He licked her, sliding his tongue across her sex and slipping it between her nether lips to probe deeper.

When his calloused finger took its place, he plied his tongue exclusively against her swollen button. Fingering her, licking, tugging at her clit, adding another digit to stretch her.

She shuddered, moaned. Writhed as her orgasm coiled, needing just a little bit more.

And that was when he stopped and stood. Wrapped his hand back in her hair and dragged her close for a kiss. She tasted herself on his mouth, and it excited her. She worked the button of his pants and opened them enough to slide her hand into his briefs.

He sucked in a breath, and she laughed, a sound he caught in a passionate kiss even as his hand slipped between their bodies to stroke her.

"Now," she panted, feeling herself on the brink. "I want to feel you inside me when I come."

"I shouldn't."

"You'd better. You can't leave me hanging. Fuck me." She intentionally used the rough word.

"Red." He moaned her nickname as the tip of his cock probed the entrance to her sex. She locked her legs around his waist and drew him closer. Deeper.

The thickness of him filled her.

Her hot breath panted against his shoulder as she clung to him.

His fingers dug into her ass as he ground himself into her.

Their bodies were joined. Meshed so tight. Her pleasure intense. When she came, he was there to catch the cry with his lips. His hips pistoned forward, thrusting so deep, drawing out the bliss.

Leaving them arched and frozen at the apex of perfection.

And someone just had to ruin it.

A voice called for her. Margaret.

Dammit. Her timing couldn't have been worse.

"How did she get in?" she whispered.

"I must not have latched the door," he murmured, his cock still semi-hard inside her. "Fuck. Want me to shoot her?"

"No." She bit her lip, lest she giggle at the preposterous idea. "Hold on, I'll get rid of her."

It meant peeling herself from Jett, her body still

tingling and flushed. She wrapped herself in a towel and fought hard not to grin like an idiot.

She'd had sex with Jett.

And it was the most amazing experience of her life.

CHAPTER FOURTEEN

What a mind-blowing encounter. What a shame that other nurse interrupted. Jett wouldn't have minded feeling Red's soft curves a little while longer. Which just went to show how far he'd fallen.

What happened to not fucking those he worked with?

And what was he thinking screwing a dying woman?

Problem was, despite what everyone kept saying, he still couldn't wrap his mind around the idea. Just a moment ago, she'd felt so alive in his arms. Passionate. Warm.

Mine.

Jett wasn't a man given to possessive thoughts, but something about her drew him. Perhaps it was best someone interrupted, lest he do something stupid like make some kind of school-boy declaration of love.

Love was for pussies. His daddy had said so every day after his mother left. Every time he downed another beer. Jett almost had it engraved on his tombstone when his pops died of liver disease seven years later. But there was a ridiculous cost for each letter. Money better spent on his own future. Even though his father's mantra never made it to stone, he remembered.

Caring made a man weak. Stupid. Apparently, he took after his father.

Grabbing his discarded shirt and pulling the damp material over his head, he drew close enough to the door to hear the murmurs of two voices. Becky yapping with that other nurse, what's her name, assigned to Chimera's pet project on level six. He'd warned the boss about the pair becoming too close, not that he'd seen them doing anything. It was just something in the way they interacted, as if they shared a secret.

I've got a secret, too. And she entered the bathroom with an exclaimed, "I thought she'd never leave."

"Did she suspect anything?"

Becky shrugged, her bare shoulders peeking from

the towel. "So what if she does? We're not doing anything wrong."

Not the first time, they hadn't. It was the fact that they continued to do it that was the problem.

It became a daily thing, him sneaking in every night, leaving before dawn every morning. Calling himself stupid each and every time. However, he couldn't seem to resist Becky. Couldn't stop thinking of her.

Another issue? His jealousy.

She entered the common room about a week after they first slept together. Leaning against a wall, sipping a coffee, he noticed the gazes tracking her. One in particular.

Mooney, that randy prick, with his Captain America good looks approached her. Jett couldn't hear what he said, but he didn't like the way she smiled. Was she flirting with him?

It roused a dark beast inside, one that screamed, "Not sharing," which might be why he was so brusque when he stalked toward her and grunted. "You need some fresh air."

"I'll take her. Keep her safe from the beasties in the woods." Moony smirked at him and almost lost his teeth.

Becky saved him from thousands in dental work.

She shook her head. "Thanks but I already asked Jett to be my escort."

She hadn't. But he appreciated the lie.

What he didn't like so much was once they got outside, the way her eyes shone and she exclaimed, "Thank you."

"For?" Not killing Mooney? He still wasn't sure he'd made the right choice.

"The flowers."

He blinked. "What flowers?"

Confusion crinkled her brow. "Wasn't it you that sent them? I got a bouquet this morning signed, your mystery admirer. I assumed it was you."

His fists clenched, almost as tight as his jaw. "Wasn't me." Who was the fucker who dared?

"Oh." She ducked her head and looked at the ground.

"I don't do that kind of shit." Never would have even occurred to him.

"That's fine. I don't need flowers. You're all I want." She placed her hand on his arm, and something wrenched inside him.

All I want.

The echo of those words was why he was out by the landing pad the next day waiting for the helicopter with its deliveries.

When she entered her room after work, it was to

find it full of rose petals, scattered on the bed. And he didn't do something so trivial as a bouquet that would die. He had a potted orchid brought in. Beautiful and delicate, just like her.

With a card that only said one thing. Jett. Which took him forever to write because words tumbled in his brain. Admissions that would make him sound weak.

But she understood. She threw herself in his arms and rode him until he bellowed her name.

Twice.

Things got more intense after that. There was no question that they spent all their free time together. He didn't even care if people noticed. He had to be with her.

Had to.

Setting himself up for a major fall because he knew they played with borrowed time. Heard it in the raspy nature of her breath as she slept. The way she sometimes would start to cough, and turn away, as if he wouldn't notice the blood in the tissues.

He had to do something. But Chimera, that sly fucking bastard, wouldn't budge. Citing side effects and her civilian status, he continued to deny her the cure.

Jett didn't give a fuck. She was dying.

And he didn't like it. But what could he do?

Get her that fucking cure. The one Chimera taunted her with. The one he refused to give. The one Jett could steal for her...

About a month after they started fucking, Jett made his move. He waited until she'd fallen asleep that night. Checked to make sure Chimera had hit his quarters, too, instead of pulling an all-nighter.

Didn't allow himself to ponder how this woman managed to worm her way into a heart he thought barren and indifferent.

Yet, the more he got to know Red, the more fascinated he found himself. Her bubbly nature in the face of impending doom...how did she manage it? How did she not rail against the world? Hate everyone and everything?

Most of all, why did the sight of him make her smile?

People didn't smile when he came striding in their direction. Most of them didn't stand their ground either, waiting for him to get close, but turned tail and ran.

It felt good to see her pleasure when he tracked her down. Felt even better when she slipped him a hug and a whispered, "Happy to see you."

Which was why, unlike her, he wasn't willing to see it end.

His access card gave him entry to the secret lab.

The fridge, the glass door lit from within in a blue electric light, beckoned. A beacon of hope.

Insanity.

If he got caught...Chimera wouldn't fire him. Jett knew too much. But he could end up in one of those cages. The ones in the back.

Jett wouldn't make a good prisoner, so at least his punishment wouldn't last long.

Only if he got caught. With his access to the cameras, it had proved easy to create a ten-minute loop. He would wipe his keycard access after the fact. Maybe set up that asshole Mooney for the fall—despite everything, that fucker kept eyeing Red in a way he didn't like. Turned out he was the bastard who'd sent her flowers. Making him look bad. Jett wouldn't mind taking him down a peg. Maybe eliminating him altogether.

Jett approached the fridge and eyed the lock. A thumbprint was needed. Chimera's print. Good thing he'd come prepared. From his pocket, he withdrew the tape and powder he'd filched. Finding a clear print proved easy in this space. Chimera's fingers had touched just about everything.

He molded the tape to his fingertip, knowing there was a strong possibility this wouldn't work. He'd only done this once before during his military days.

Would it work again?

He pressed it against the lock.

Nothing happened.

He shoved his finger against it again and again.

The fridge didn't open. And a voice said, "It won't unlock for you."

Whirling, he beheld Chimera standing in the shadows, having arrived from who the fuck knew where.

Some people might have bluffed their way out. Jett wasn't that kind of pussy. He owned his shit. "I want the cure for cancer."

"Are you ill?"

"Not for me. For her."

"By her I assume you mean Nurse Frederickson." Chimera stepped closer, enough the blue glow from the fridge slanted across his countenance, giving it sharp planes and shadows.

"Doesn't seem fair that you've got a cure right here and you're letting her die."

"Am I?" The man arched a brow. "Just because I'm not openly feeding her a cure doesn't mean I'm doing nothing."

"Meaning?"

"Meaning I'm trying to subtly shift your lady friend without drawing her attention. Too fast and she'll notice."

"Too slow and she might still die."

Chimera shrugged. "Also a possibility."

"If you're healing her, then why is she looking worse?"

"Her body is in a radical fight. Do you really think it's going to be easy?"

No. But it pained Jett to see her losing weight. Noticing the circles under her eyes. More than one night he'd held her as she thrashed in the grips of a nightmare.

"Why not tell her?" She would owe her life to the clinic, to Chimera.

"Because she still has those journals. The ones where she's been recording her observations of me, the clinic. Everyone."

Jett snorted. "And? Would take two seconds to burn them."

"She aspires to be a journalist. This would be the story of a lifetime. I don't think that will stop her from telling the world about us."

"I think she'd trade a big scoop for a second chance."

"Would she?" Chimera's gaze narrowed. "I thought that of others, and yet the first chance they get, they betray me." The pointed look zeroed in on Jett.

But he'd done too many things bad things in his

life to feel guilt. "Maybe if you'd told me you were doing something, I wouldn't have had to go behind your back."

"And maybe you should trust me more. How long have we worked together?"

"Awhile."

"In all that time, you have never shown a romantic interest in anyone."

"What are you talking about? I fuck plenty when I go to town."

"Fuck, yes. Care, no. Did you think I wouldn't notice and help the one person I know is loyal to my cause?"

"In other words, I'm a dick for not trusting you."

"It's not your fault. You're human." Chimera turned to stare at the vials in the fridge.

Yes, Jett was human. As opposed to... Not for the first time, Jett wondered just what Chimera had done to himself. He knew that the man used to suffer from some debilitating disease, the kind that broke the body and put him in a wheelchair. Chimera became his very first experiment. A successful one by most indications, but what kind of balls—or desperation—did it take to inject yourself with an unproven drug?

"Will she"—start biting people at random, grow a tail, glow in the dark—"have any side effects?"

"She shouldn't. I've been treating her with the same stuff we used on that senator and the European prince."

He knew of whom Chimera spoke. Success cases who, to the world at large, appeared as miraculous recoveries.

"Thank you."

"It's I who should thank you. You've been a good man, Jett. A loyal man. Think of this as a reward."

A damned good reward.

He felt a lot better snuggling her that night. Spooning her into his body. Ignoring the rattle of her breath.

Chimera was fixing her. Yet, a tiny part of him wondered, did he lie?

CHAPTER FIFTEEN

"I think you should stay in bed." Jett didn't creep out at dawn for once, which meant, when she emerged from the bathroom after an epic coughing fit, he stood there, looking like he wanted to kill something.

If only he could slay her disease.

"I am only staying in bed if you are. Naked, I should add."

"Can't. But you don't sound good. Tell Chimera you need a day off."

"Not happening. Especially since I feel fine." She hoped he wouldn't recognize the lie. This past week, she'd felt herself getting worse.

"Bullshit. You look like crap."

"Gee, thanks."

"And your cough is getting worse." He frowned. "Maybe you should see a doctor."

"No doctors. I'm just a little tired. Bad dreams again." Dreams of drowning. "Nothing a coffee won't fix. What I won't be able to fix is the problem we'll have if someone sees you in these halls. No boys allowed remember." A rule that was much laxer than she'd been led to believe.

"Someone says anything, and they'll regret it."

She rolled her eyes. "Save the macho act. We don't need to get in trouble. Shoo. I'll see you later." She shoved him toward the door, hoping he didn't sense the urgency in the act.

Jett left before the tickle in her throat sent her running for the bathroom. The coughing lasted a good several minutes, the red splatter in her sink a chilling reminder. It seemed her chest was always tight these days, gurgling with fluid. Her doctor's hopeful prediction of six months was proving overly optimistic. The pain meds she'd scored were helping, but she took more and more each day. Jett didn't know.

She couldn't tell him even as she knew it wasn't fair. Why did she have to find him now? The one man who completed her. A man she'd soon have to leave so that he remembered her only during the good times.

Upon emerging from her room, a shiver gripped her, a deep chill that had settled in her bones. She wondered if she should grab a thicker sweater for work. She was so cold. Always cold.

How much longer did she have?

Not long enough. The funny thing about regret was she'd not truly felt any until recently. Until Jett.

It wasn't even as if the man had said anything to her. Certainly not the L word. In public, he remained surly and unsmiling. He ate with her but scowled at anyone who looked their way. She'd leaned over one day and asked him, *"Is there a reason why you're shooting eye lasers at everyone?"*

"Fuckers are staring at you."

"Of course, they are because they're wondering how you managed to scoop the cutest nurse in this place."

"Because my dick is bigger than theirs."

"Jett!" she exclaimed, her cheeks heating.

His slow sexy smile just about melted her. "What? It's the truth."

"You're so bad."

"Yup."

He didn't deny it, and she wasn't under any illusions about him. Jett had violent tendencies. A surly attitude. A mocking disrespect of others. But with her...he was a different man. One who gifted her with the most amazing smile, acerbic sense of humor, a need to pleasure her, and made her feel...

"Becky?" The query startled her, and she jumped. How long had she stood mooning in the hallway? She turned to face Margaret, a woman she'd not seen in awhile.

Margaret's expression bespoke her shock. At times Becky barely recognized herself, the woman in the mirror a shrunken version of herself. Which made her wonder why Jett stuck around.

The conversation started off on the wrong foot, with Margaret gasping, "What happened to you?"

"I don't know what you mean." Becky pulled the door to her room shut then hugged her sweater more tightly around her body. As if that would somehow hide her wasting body.

"You look exhausted."

"Probably because I am." She rolled her shoulders. "It happens. I've been working long hours and not sleeping well."

"Is everything okay?"

"I'm fine. Just having some weird nightmares." Terrifying ones that woke her in a cold sweat.

"About?" Margaret seemed genuinely concerned, and for a moment, Becky remembered the friendship they used to share before they both started getting too involved in their work. Before Becky started keeping secrets.

"I've been dreaming about water. Lots of water. With me in it." Becky's lips twisted. "Which is crazy because I don't swim."

"Good thing. That lake is dangerous."

Margaret wasn't the first to mention it. She'd heard many warnings about the deceptive depth, the cold, and then the other rumors of things living in the water.

"I heard you fell in and almost drowned." If it hadn't been for the quick actions of Margaret's patient, she would have died. At times, when the pain got bad, Becky wondered if that was what the dreams were predicting. Drowning because of the cancer filling her lungs.

"I didn't fall," Maggie blurted.

"So what, someone pushed you?" Had Maggie's patient shoved her in and then saved her?

Margaret shook her head. "Something in the water yanked me in."

The words reminded Becky too much of her dream. The one where arms wrapped around her and dragged her down. "Do you remember what it looked like?" she asked in all seriousness.

"I didn't really see it. It felt like a tentacle,

though, wrapped around me. But what kind of lake creature has one? Octopuses live in the oceans."

"There's all kinds of things in this world we've never discovered. Could be the Ogopogo." Becky had studied up on legends since coming here. Trying to sort fact from fiction.

"Lake monster?" Margaret wrinkled her nose, and her expression said what she thought.

Becky stiffened. "It's possible. The lake is deep and could have something never seen before. Scientists find new species every year."

"Of course, they do. I didn't mean to say it wasn't possible. Dr. Chimera says I imagined it."

"Dr. Chimera says a lot of thing. But keep in mind he has secrets." So many secrets.

"That's what Luke says."

"Ah yes, your miracle patient who recovered. I've seen him around. I can see why you didn't mind playing nursemaid." At times Becky missed dealing with real people. The rats didn't seem to like her. Chimera wasn't exactly the friendly sort when they worked. A good thing she had Jett.

"I wasn't the one who chose the job," Margaret replied.

"Wonder what they'll have you doing now that he's all better."

"I'm sure they'll find me something to do."

"Speaking of doing, I should get back to work."

"Take care of yourself, Becky. You really do look run down. Maybe you should ask for some time off."

Time off would be admitting the sickness was winning. She wouldn't allow it. Couldn't.

"I don't need a break." Becky shook her head and then, because she couldn't help herself, "You're just saying that because you're jealous I'm working closely with Dr. Chimera. You want to take my place."

"I'm worried about you is all. Maybe you should see about getting some vitamins or something. Have you been getting fresh air?"

"I don't need you worrying about me." A lie. She wanted someone to care, but if she told Maggie how sick she was, she'd have to deal with her pity. "I'm fine. All good. I just came to grab a sweater. I'm going for a walk."

"Do you want me to come with you?"

Becky heard the undertone. *You're weak. You need help.*

And the worst part? It was true. The problem remained. Nothing could fix what ailed her. Probably too late even for Chimera's magic serums.

She took off, making her turn outside short. The fresh air only served to aggravate her lungs.

Soon enough, she was in Dr. Chimera's secret

lab, eyeing the locked fridge with the various remedies. She'd once asked him why there were so many
different ones.

"Because everyone has a different need." She still
remembered him pointing to a lovely aquamarine
one with a silvery sheen, the same one he'd shown
her before. "That one might one day cure asthma."
He then indicated a green one. "Skin regeneration."
The purple one might be a cure for heart disease.
Yellow, the liver.

Not for the first time, she wondered what would
happen if she got a hold of the cure. Would a full vial
be enough? Or would one dose be like trying to put
out a blazing inferno with a tiny water pistol?

The rats didn't need much of the fluids for the
tumors to shrink. But they were tiny in comparison
to her. She'd pricked herself one day when Chimera
wasn't watching and the cameras were down for
maintenance. The tiny amount she took didn't have
enough in it to make a difference.

What if she could get more? She eyed the rack of
the cure in the fridge.

Go big or go home. Auntie never did believed in
half measures. However, taking even a single vial
would be noticed. The cameras in the lab watched
her every move. Even if she did score a vial, would
one be enough?

The list of tasks Chimera had left included more rat testing. The new batch of rodents delivered only a few days before appeared perfectly healthy. She had no idea what was in the pink serum she injected half of them with. Asking Chimera meant getting a boisterous, "Revolutionary stuff." Which explained nothing.

She spent a moment preparing her tray. Prefilling the syringes. Getting her alcohol swabs ready. Putting on gloves. Dealing with rats wasn't her idea of a good time. They freaked her out with their beady eyes and fleshy tails.

With her station prepped, she wheeled the cart over to the cages at the back. The rats inside stopped what they were doing to sit on their haunches and glare.

Yes, glare, their whiskers not moving as they watched her every move. Probably smelling the death oozing from her skin and cheering it on.

Jett claimed it was her imagination. She begged to differ when those red orbs zeroed in on her.

Hating them, though, didn't mean she would neglect her tasks.

"Okay, Bertha. You're first," she murmured as she coaxed the white rat over into a different cage via a tunnel.

Bertha didn't even wait for Becky to lower a treat

to tempt her. She scurried into the empty cage and sat, little paws clasped, as if she knew what was expected of her. For all Becky knew, the rat did understand. Who knew what kind of cognition these injections gave them

She dropped the wall that sealed off the tunnel then lifted the door to the cage and reached in. Bertha didn't move and allowed Becky to grab her. She lifted her out of the cage.

"Sorry about this." She apologized every time. Unable to stand the staring red eyes.

As she brought the needle near, Bertha acted. She whipped her head around and chomped on Becky's hand. The latex gloves did nothing to stop the stinging pain. Becky gasped, and her fingers reflexively spasmed, releasing the rat, who landed on the cage.

Not that Becky cared about the rat. Blood welled up through the incisions left by its teeth.

"Oh shoot." She ran for the sink and the disinfectant kept alongside it. A fierce scrubbing followed by the application of antibacterial cream and a bandage took care of the bleeding bite. It took only a few minutes.

When she turned away from the sink, it was to blink uncomprehendingly. The rats, every single one of them, sat outside the cage. Staring at her.

That can't be good.

"How did you get out?" she whispered. Because the cage door was closed. She never touched it. Yet now it hung open. And sitting beside it?

Bertha.

"Did you do that?" she asked, planting her hands on her hips. "Dr. Chimera is going to be giddy if it turns out he made you smart."

The cameras would have caught what happened. And now she had to catch those rats, or at least as many as possible, before they escaped.

"Back into the cage now. I've got cheese," she sang, pulling out a chunk from her pocket and waving it.

The rats didn't appear to care and turned to look at Bertha. The furry shake of a head had Becky gaping.

"Did you just say no?" She waggled the hand with the treat. "But it's cheese. You love cheese."

Apparently, Bertha liked freedom more. She hissed before leaping to the floor, her rodent friends swarming behind her.

"Get back over here." The escaping rodents didn't listen. They swarmed to a ventilation grill alongside a locked door—hiding a room she'd never seem. They managed to squeeze their bodies through the honeycomb holes, leaving Becky alone and wondering where the rats would end up.

I might want to find some mousetraps. Just in case they went looking for revenge and found the ventilation duct to her room. It would suck to wake up to them chewing on her face.

She headed for the intercom, knowing she had to page Dr. Chimera. She pressed the button and said, "Tell the doctor there's been an incident."

"What kind?" his secretary asked.

"Rodent escape."

"We'll send someone down to catch it."

"Might not be that easy. It wasn't one of them, but all of them. And they got into the ventilation system."

"Oh dear." The line went dead.

When it opened again, Chimera barked, "The rats escaped! How? I thought I told you to never open the main cage."

"I didn't." Then, despite knowing how crazy it sounded, said, "I think Bertha figured out how to open it."

"It worked." The breathed words reinforced her belief. Chimera was playing with their intelligence.

"I don't know what worked, but I can tell you they escaped and are at this moment somewhere in the ducts, doing who knows what."

"I'll be right down."

The call ended, and she leaned against the wall beside it. Her tray of tools still sat beside the cages. The syringes and their pink fluid unused. Not even tempting. She didn't need more brains.

She pushed off from the wall and decided she might as well get the stuff put away. As she neared the far wall, and the grill the rats escaped via, she heard it.

A distant roar.

What on Earth? She crouched down and eyed the grill. She half expected to see beady red eyes staring back. Nothing appeared. She chalked it up to her imagination and was about to rise when she heard it again. The brutish snorts of an animal.

Did Chimera keep something bigger than a rat in that hidden room? As far as she knew he didn't have permission to experiment with larger mammals. Not even chimps. So what was hiding in there?

She stood and frowned at the door. The doctor had never let her see inside. Yet, more than once, he'd emerged from there when she worked.

She took a step closer to the door, knowing it would be locked. The doctor alone entered it, using a palm print rather than a key card.

The intercom in the room crackled. "Get out."

She rolled her eyes. "The rats are gone. I'm fine."

"Get out, Red. Now." The panic in Jett's voice caught her attention. She turned to look at the camera in the ceiling, knowing he watched.

What had him panicked?

Click.

Her eyes widened as she heard the lock on the door to the hidden room disengage. Had the doctor been inside all this time?

The portal opened, a thick metal thing meant to withstand quite a bit of force. Probably because what stood behind it needed a sturdy prison door.

"Ohmygod." She froze in place as she stared at the monster in front of her. And yes, monster was the only word. Seven feet tall, thick, and bullish in features, the thing stared around wildly before focusing on her.

"Eep." Self-preservation kicked in, and she ran for the other door, only it didn't budge. A robotic voice said, "Lockdown initiated."

Lockdown? But she was in here with a monster. She whirled at the sound of destruction, only to see the minotaur-like beast rampaging around the room. Grabbing hold of machines and tossing them. Sweeping counters clear. Since he seemed more intent on breaking than killing, she dove out of sight, scrambling to hide behind a counter, doing her best to hold her breath.

Yet the tickle in her throat betrayed her.

She couldn't help but cough and, in the silence that followed, prayed to every god that had ignored her thus far.

A warm puff of air hit the top of her head. She tilted her head up and saw the open maw of the monster.

And screamed!

CHAPTER SIXTEEN

Jett ran for the lab, wishing he could move faster. Why did it have to be so far? A room and a hall away didn't seem like a great distance until someone was in danger.

Then there was the fact the lab had gone into lockdown mode. His keycard wouldn't work.

He slammed his fist on the door, the rocky surface, helping with its camouflage, grating skin. "Open, dammit." How could he save Becky if he couldn't reach her?

The walkie-talkie at his belt crackled. "Where are you?" Chimera asked.

"Locked out of the tunnel, goddammit. I need to get in."

"I'm coming."

"I don't need you here. I need the door to fucking open."

"We can't let the subject escape."

"I wasn't planning to." He glared at the wall in his way.

"You can't kill him either."

"Now you're pushing your luck."

The pounding of steps had him glancing over his shoulder as Chimera, looking more frantic than usual, joined him. "We need to lure the subject into the hall and trigger the gas vents."

"Easy enough. Open the inner lab door and let him through." If escape were the main focus of the subject, then he'd enter easily enough.

"Give me a second." Chimera stuck his hand through the hologram, and a moment later, it was gone. The console flashed red, and the glow reflected against Chimera's face as he tapped on it.

"Inner lab door is open." Chimera tapped the screen, and they could see a video of the hall.

It took a moment, a moment of anxiety because Jett had no idea what was happening in the lab. No idea if Red was okay.

And his first glimpse of her, slung over the monster's shoulder, made his blood run cold. "He's got Becky."

"And?" Chimera stood with his finger poised

over the button to slam the door shut and activate the gas.

"And you'll fucking kill her if you use the vents." Jett shoved Chimera aside.

"What would you suggest I do?" the doctor snapped. "Ask him to place her inside the lab, pretty please."

"Let me in." Jett pointed to the door. "Let me in and I'll handle it."

"You'll kill it."

"I'll kill you first if you don't open the fucking door." A threat he'd probably regret later. Yet, what choice did he have? Becky needed him.

"You're being foolish. She's just a nurse."

"A nurse that you know I'm fucking. So open the goddamned door!" he roared.

"Try not to kill him." Chimera tapped, and there was an audible click as the door slid open. Jett wasted no time and dove through, ignoring the thud as the hall sealed shut behind him.

Exactly what possessed him to get into a confined space with an adrenalized monster?

Oh yeah. The tiny woman hanging over the brute's shoulder.

"Hey there, ugly. Mind putting the female down and talking this over?" Jett hadn't pulled his weapon yet. No point in spooking the thing until he had to.

The monster opened his mouth and bellowed. Even further gone than Jorge, he'd lost the ability to speak. Which meant this would happen the hard way.

"I'm afraid blaaaargh isn't the right answer." Jett held out his hands. "Come on, dude. You need to get past me if you want to go through that door." He jerked his head.

That seemed to do it. The monster yanked her down and dropped her at his feet. Distracted by the fact that Becky immediately scrabbled away from the thing, Jett almost missed the monster moving. Good thing he reacted quickly.

Jett ducked, leaning his shoulder forward enough that when the monster whipped out ham-sized fists, they missed, but Jett connected. He used his body as a fulcrum to topple the monster. Even as he heard the thump, he whirled, kicked out, his foot lifting to smash the beast in the nose.

It roared.

Jett roared back. Not exactly the same effect, but it helped in a fight. Boiled the blood and fired the adrenaline. He charged at the man—forever changed by science—and again ducked under the wildly swinging punches.

It helped that the patient lacked any true skill.

Any one of those blows would have broken Jett. Since he had orders not to kill, he had to disarm.

In a fight where you could be killed, there was no such thing as dirty, hence why he felt no compunction about nailing the monster in the nut sac .

Like every male in the world, he bellowed, cupped, and hit the floor. Jett didn't relent. He pounced on top, grabbed his gun, and fired all the darts into the beast.

Not enough. He found himself flying as the monster shoved him.

He hit the wall and slumped down, but only for a second.

With the tranquilizer having failed—meaning Chimera needed to invest in stronger drugs for the future—there weren't many options left.

He bolted to the far end of the hall and grabbed hold of Becky, dragging her upright. "Open it!" he yelled. Hoping Chimera would see his lips and understand his intent.

It occurred to him, too fucking late, that Chimera could easily activate the gas and take all three of them out. It would certainly be easiest.

The beast roared from the far end of the hall. He began his charge, a bull rushing in. The door clicked, and Jett stumbled into the lab with Becky.

"Hide," he ordered as he whipped around. He

saw nothing he could use to stop the beast, whose eyes glared with red malevolence.

Just when he feared he'd have to resort to grabbing a stool and clubbing the creature, the door slid shut.

The monster hit it with a hard thud. *Bang. Thump.* Despite the thickness, the door dimpled with the hits.

And then there was silence.

"Thank fuck that's over," he said with a sigh.

"My hero!" Becky's arms wrapped around him tight, and he closed his eyes in relief.

Red lived.

But it was close.

Too close. And he'd not forgotten the fact that Chimera thought her expendable.

He tightened the embrace, enjoying the feel of her against him, then set her away from him for a shake. "I told you to get the fuck out! Why didn't you listen?"

Rather than reply, she asked a question of her own. "What was that thing?"

He pressed his lips tight.

"Jett?"

"Nothing. Forget what you saw." Because he was all too aware cameras watched and recorded everything he said. Or did they? He noticed the camera above the door was gone. Ripped free and smashed on the floor. But there could be others.

"Did Chimera do that to him? It? Was that a person?"

He ignored her rapid-fire queries to stick his head through the door that was usually kept locked. Noted the cage holding the patient opened wide. Fucking rats. They'd streamed out of a vent and gone straight to it. What he couldn't figure out was, why? They'd managed to escape. Yet they'd taken a detour to free a patient. He stepped farther into the room, scanning the crevices and corners. Despite Chimera's thoughts on the matter, if he saw red beady eyes, he'd kick them.

Becky followed. "I am talking to you. The least you could do is reply."

"I can't reply because there's nothing to say." He cast her a glance that he hoped she'd understand. One that said, stop talking about it.

She blinked at him. Then smiled. "You don't have to. I totally understand now."

"What's that supposed to mean?"

She glanced around, the empty cages much too large for the smaller animals usually used by science. "Nothing. Forget I said anything." She swept out of the room, and it was his turn to follow.

"You can't talk about this," he reiterated.

"Of course not."

"I'm serious, Red. No one must ever know what you've seen here."

"Who would believe me?" Her lips tilted. "I mean, do you know how crazy it would sound if I claimed a minotaur rampaged through the lab and tried to kidnap me? Where was he taking me anyhow? And why?"

"Doesn't matter. You're safe."

As if the word triggered it, reality and shock finally hit her. "Oh God. He was going to kill me."

"If you were lucky." There was a reason that patient had ended up in the secret lab. The last nurse he'd gotten his hands on still screamed at the slightest touch.

"I think I'm going to be sick." The statement she made before she threw herself into his arms. Once more he hugged her. Hugged her tight, thankful he'd arrived in time. Thankful for one more day with Red.

There were things he wanted to say to her. However, there was no time to talk. No time for anything as the door opened and Chimera swept in exclaiming, "My poor lab!"

CHAPTER SEVENTEEN

WHEN CHIMERA ENTERED, JETT SLIPPED FREE and adopted his serious mien, so Becky hugged herself. Anything to hide the tremors in her body.

She'd almost died, and the thing was she thought she'd come to grips with it. After all, a bomb ticked inside her body. Yet, when given the choice, she realized she wanted to live. Even better, Jett wanted her to live, too. He'd confronted a monster to save her.

My hero.

A man who fought a beast single handedly. A thing that shouldn't even exist.

A monster hid in the locked room adjacent to the lab. No wonder the doctor had never allowed her a peek. Chimera had lied when he claimed to be aboveboard and following the rules. The rats he had her playing with were just a clever cover. The hidden room with the cages was the reality, the scoop she'd been searching for, and now she'd seen the proof.

As she puttered around the destroyed lab, she heard snippets as Jett relayed to Chimera what had happened.

The smart rats were to blame. They'd entered the secret room and opened the cage with the beast.

Why? Who knew? Perhaps like Pinky and the Brain they wanted to rule the world. Whatever the case, the result proved catastrophic, the damage extensive with counters wiped clean of beakers and equipment. Broken glass littered the floor. The fridge, with all of its colorful samples, lay on its side, the door popped open. So many spilled fluids forming a rainbow-hued puddle.

"Fuck." Chimera glared at the mess as he exited the hall. A glance past him showed Jett directing the guards carrying off the sleeping beast.

"What was that thing?" she asked.

"None of your business," Chimera snapped. "If you hadn't let the rats escape, this wouldn't have happened."

Her shoulders straightened at the rebuke. "I'm not to blame for what was in *that* room." She pointed. "I thought it was going to kill me."

"It didn't. And you're lucky my subject is still

alive." His harangue bit, especially since the intent was clear.

That thing is more important than me.

It meant she had a saucy reply. "I don't know if he'd agree about the lucky part. He didn't seem too happy. What did you do to him?"

"Don't take that tone with me."

"I'll take whatever damned tone I like given I'm the one who almost died because you"—she jabbed a finger—"were hiding things from me. The least you can do is offer an explanation and apology."

Rather than blow up and give Becky her marching orders, Chimera rubbed his face and sighed. "Sorry. You are correct. I shouldn't be sniping at you. It's not your fault. It's mine for not realizing the potential in the new intelligence enhancer. Please forgive my boorish accusations."

The apology didn't quite explain things, and a part of her wanted to push. Demand answers. However, as her auntie always said, free drinks were more likely with an unbuttoned blouse. With Jett hovering, she couldn't exactly pull on her feminine wiles, nor did she want to; however, it did make her try another tact.

"Apology accepted. And how exciting you've made a breakthrough."

"Have I?" Chimera looked sadly at the mess of

fluid on the floor. "The samples we were using are gone. Months of work lost."

"Not everything was broken." She knelt among the wreckage. "We can save some of the serums." She reached for an unbroken pink one and shook it at him.

The doctor's face brightened. "We'll have to act quickly. I don't know how the compounds will react if left unrefrigerated for long."

"Then we'd better get moving. Think the kitchen has room for them? Or the labs on level three?" She made the suggestions knowing he'd reject them.

"No. They're much too valuable for those unsecured locations. But we can borrow one of their fridges." Chimera rubbed his chin. "While I go see about a new cooling unit, you gather the intact vials. But be careful not to cut yourself on those shards. We don't want an unfortunate incident. Wear gloves," he admonished. "Once we've rescued the undamaged serums, then we'll call in maintenance to handle the rest of the mess."

Chimera left, and she began fishing out the vials from the wreckage, placing them gently in a box that she found dumped on the floor. She took Chimera's advice to heart and wore two layers of gloves but, even so, was very careful to avoid sharp edges. Most of the vials in the back of the fridge survived intact, including the majority of the aquamarine ones. The ones he said were for healing lungs.

She fingered one wondering if it had caused the monster in the back. That *thing* was living proof of the experimental nature of what Chimera did. Was it once a man, or a beast genetically modified like the rats?

She had no way of knowing, just like she had no way of discerning if this vial would cure her cancer. Did she dare experiment on herself?

Did she have a choice? She was dying.

The cure might be in the palm of her hands.

It could also kill her.

She thought of Jett. Of how she felt with him. Of the fear when she thought she might die. She glanced around, noting no one remained in the lab. All the guards, including Jett, had left with the minotaur. A peek overheard was mostly to reassure herself the camera remained gone. Only loose wires dangled from the ceiling. No one watched.

No one would know.

Before she could think twice, she pocketed the vials, five of them, leaving behind three, which she placed in the box with the others. Just in time as Chimera returned, Jett behind him, wheeling a fridge on a dolly.

His dark gaze flicked over her, and she flushed, wondering if he could read the guilt on her face.

"I put the unbroken ones over there." She pointed to the counter with the box of rainbow-colored vials.

"Thank you." Chimera let out a sigh of frustration. "Months of work ruined. But on a more positive note, the brain enhancer worked. So I guess we can't call it a complete loss."

"It actually made them smarter?" she asked.

"It did. Can you imagine the applications?" the doctor replied.

Jett interrupted, wagging his walkie-talkie. "Maintenance is here to finish cleanup."

"Let them in. Then take Ms. Frederickson to her quarters. She looks exhausted."

"I'm fine. I don't need an escort." She didn't want anyone with her when she did the unthinkable.

But Jett didn't take orders from her. He escorted her, expression grim, body tense. He said not a word, and neither did she.

He knew. He knew and disapproved.

The moment they entered her quarters she expected a harangue. Instead, she found herself pressed against a wall. His mouth hotly latching to hers. His motions frenetic with need.

"What's wrong?" she asked.

"You almost died." Said roughly. His voice tight with emotion.

She cradled his cheek, enjoying the roughness of the shadow. "I will die. Maybe not today, but it's coming." Soon, if the hidden vials didn't do the trick.

She thought he might say something. A declaration of, if not love, then the fact he cared. But Jett wasn't one to use words. He showed her.

He dipped his head and claimed her lips, softly this time. He coaxed, teasing her bottom lip until she parted them with a content sigh.

When her arms laced around him, clasping him tight, he gave a grunt. His happy grunt. He also pressed her body firmly against his. Branding her. Igniting her passion.

A desire that couldn't be contained.

He was right. She'd almost died. Which made this moment, this intimacy all the more precious because, how many more of these moments would they have?

She kissed him back, not content to take things slow and sensual. She grasped his shoulders, digging in her fingers as sensual fire consumed her body.

"You're wearing too many things," he grumbled.

"So are you." A problem quickly fixed, leaving them naked, the heated flesh of their bodies able to rub as they continued to kiss. His tongue slipped into her mouth for a taste. A glide of wetness and then a suck that made her knees buckle.

But he was there to catch her. He lifted her off the floor, pushing her back against the wall. Her legs wrapped around his waist and drew him close, close enough he could grind his pelvis against hers, his cock trapped between their bodies, the hardness of it rubbing against her slick sex. The friction proved delicious, and she couldn't help but moan and demand more.

"Now, Jett. Please. I want to feel you inside me," she murmured. "Need you."

With a groan, his hips shifted, freeing his cock. The tip of him probed, pushing at her slit. She locked her legs tight and drew him in. Gasping as the thickness of him stretched her.

Filled her.

He took her standing, the thrust of his body against hers bringing gasps of pleasure.

"Fuck me, Red. You feel so fucking good." The words spilled from him, a moment before his lips caught hers for a torrid kiss.

Their tongues dueled as he pushed deeper into her, grinding himself, drawing the most delicious sensations. She held him tight, arms and legs wrapped around, sucking at his tongue, nibbling at his lips.

His hips pulled back, teasing her with only the tip of his dick. She wanted him sheathed, so she tightened her legs and slammed him back in.

"Jeezus, Red." Jett threw his head back, the cords in his neck bulging with the strain of controlling himself.

But she wanted him wild. Wanted him to lose himself inside her.

"Fuck me," she whispered, knowing the vulgar words would excite him.

The reaction was instantaneous. He shifted his grip, gripping her around the thighs, spreading her wide that he might pump her hard and fast. He slammed his cock in and out of her, deep strokes. Hard thrusts.

She cried out and clawed at him as her channel gripped him tight.

"Yes. Yes." She panted as he kept slamming into her, his motions frantic. His control lost.

When he changed the angle, he hit her G-spot, and it took only a few strokes before it was all over for her. She came.

Came with a shudder and a cry of his name. Her moist flesh pulsing around his cock, squeezing him tight.

"Red." He sighed her name as he came, spilling

inside her. He caught her lips in a soft kiss, a kiss that she wanted to last forever.

But he couldn't stay. His walkie-talkie went off before they'd caught their breath, and he growled, "I've got to go."

He returned late that night, angry, his steps brisk as he paced her room.

"What's wrong?" she asked, her voice thick with sleep.

"Boss is making me head to the city."

That woke her up. "What? When? Why?"

"Tonight. And I can't say any more than that." He sighed. "Fuck me. I don't want to go."

She didn't want him to leave either and yet... without him here, she could go through with her desperate plan.

"Don't worry about me. I'll be fine." Could he hear the lie?

"But I'll miss you." The words wrenched out of him, and her heart almost broke, especially since she didn't know what would happen, or if she would even be around when he returned.

"Come here." She held open her arms, and he came into them, his body heavy, his kisses fierce. He took her quickly, bringing her to orgasm with his mouth then again with his cock. Leaving her panting in bed, the scent of him on her sheets. Sheets that grew cold with his departure.

But it was for the best. The vials and their possible miracle cure called to her. Teased her with the possibilities.

The question was, one at a time or all at once?

Despite her eagerness, she chose to do one per day.

One per day for five days.

Days during which she had no one to talk to. Jett had been shipped off on a helicopter to handle some mysterious business with Mr. Lowry. All he managed was a brief video call, where he took in her appearance and said, "You look like shit."

Her reply? "Because I miss you."

She took comfort in the concern in his gaze. His whispered, "Stay safe. I'll be back as soon as I can."

Soon stretched from five days to seven. The vials were all gone, and her lungs still hurt. Even more than before.

The ache in her heart, though, was his fault. She missed him. Missed not having anyone to talk to. Especially as the nightmares grew intense, leaving her shivering and shaking, covered in sweat. Was this the cancer or the serum at work?

She wished she had someone to ask. She didn't even have Margaret anymore. After their last encounter, the woman had up and disappeared overnight. The rumor mill claimed she was let go due to management differences. But given Luke, Margaret's one and only patient, appeared to have disappeared at the same time, she wondered.

Did they run off together?

Whatever the reason, Becky missed her. Wished she'd been nicer those last few times because she could have used a friend. Especially now.

Something is wrong with me. And she didn't think the cancer was to blame. Seeing her looking wan, Chimera had told her to take the day off and rest. Sleep wouldn't fix what ailed her. Perhaps fresh air would.

Heading outside, she winced at the bright light. Coughed at the briskness of the fresh air. Still, she didn't go back inside. Her steps took her to the shore of the lake, where she shivered despite the warm rays of the sun. For the past few days she'd been running a fever. A cold one, which made no sense. Her core temperature kept dropping, and her skin itched. Itched something fierce.

She also craved water. Not to drink. Nope. She wanted to soak in it. Took crazy long showers that never quite satisfied. She wanted a bath. A way to submerge her whole body, hence why the lake drew her.

The large body of water had always intimidated her. Yet it kept calling. Even in her dreams she saw it.

As if in a trance, she kicked off her shoes and stepped into the water. The cold barely registered, but a sense of relief swept her.

More. She needed more. So she waded deeper and deeper until the bottom dropped away and she began to sink. Like a rock.

And she did nothing to stop it. Panic only began to claw at her as her lungs tightened. The pressure in them built. Begged. Screamed for her to breathe.

She convulsed and flailed, suddenly realizing what had happened.

I'm drowning. Oh God. What have I done?

She began kicking, only to find herself being dragged down by the weight of her clothes. The last of the air left her body, and she floated, eyes wide open, still drifting downwards. How deep was this lake?

From above, parts of it could be seen clear as day, but she'd chosen to walk into the darker section where the bottom lay out of sight. Yet she could still see.

Her body cried out for air. Yet there was none to be found. Her lungs were desperate for her to breathe. Any moment now she'd officially drown, which sucked.

I don't want to die.

Not yet. So many things she'd yet to do. Bungee jump. Eat a real poutine from Quebec. Snorkel in the tropics. Get white sand in the crotch of her bathing suit. Tell Jett she loved him.

Too late for that.

She heaved in a breath, a lungful of water that would end it all.

The cold fluid filled her lungs. She blinked and waited to die.

Didn't die right away. What the heck? Since her lungs hurt again, she blew out, noticed the little bubbles rising from her mouth and heaved in another breath.

She noticed something odd. Her lungs no longer hurt, and she found herself inhaling water and expelling it as if it were air. How was this possible?

She tried to talk.

"Blrgergrg." The sound was muffled and indecipherable.

Did she dream?

Something nudged her. Startled, she turned in the water, only then realizing she'd stopped her sinking and floated. She came face to face with a fish. A big fish. It nudged her again.

"Shhpptt." The garbled warning to stop did nothing to halt the fish from poking at her again, the touch of him cold and scaly.

But it gave her an idea. Didn't dolphins save people all the time? She wrapped her arms around the fish before she could think twice. Only to blow out a stream of water in shock as it bolted.

Straight down. Deeper. Away from the light.

Away from it all.

CHAPTER EIGHTEEN

"No, that can't be right." Jett made them rewind the footage and watched again. And again, as Becky walked to the edge of the lake and then waded in. Waded until her head went under.

She never came back up.

He punched the wall, the pain of hitting concrete not enough to numb the pain suddenly filling his heart.

Why? Why had she done that?

Had his leaving been the catalyst? Or had she taken a turn for the worse?

Whatever the reason, she'd chosen to suicide by drowning.

And he was fucking sad about it. Actually sad didn't come close to covering his emotions. Yeah, fucking emotions because he cared for Becky. The way she smiled, no matter how much he scowled. The way she chattered, not always expecting a reply, yet when he did talk, she listened to him intently.

The way she lit up when she saw him. Melted at his touch. Hugged him close as if he mattered.

His eyes prickled, and it shocked to realize the loss of her brought him to tears.

Guess I liked her more than I knew. More than he'd ever admitted. Which meant he felt guilty. Perhaps he should have told her how much he actually cared for her. Sure, it was emasculating, but the woman was fucking dying. And he couldn't even give her that?

What he wouldn't give to have one last chance to tell her how he felt.

Instead, all he could do was drown his sorrows with a bottle of vodka, which he drank along the shore of the lake. Toasting the woman who'd managed to make a killer feel.

No wonder his dad advised against it. Caring hurt. Hurt in a way no stab wound or gunshot ever managed.

The crunch of footsteps roused a snarled and slurred, "Fuck off."

"You're taking her death awfully hard."

"She was a nice girl. And you"—he turned a

bleary glare on his boss—"let her die. You could have saved her. You said you were healing her."

"I was trying. A pity she couldn't wait. Probably for the best, given what she saw."

"I could have convinced her to stay quiet," Jett muttered, taking another slug of burning alcohol.

"Maybe you could have. But what about when you tired of her? It would have happened, don't deny it."

Thing was Jett *did* want to deny it. Did Chimera really not grasp just how rare his affection for Becky was?

"Doesn't matter now, does it? She's gone." No more teasing or touching. Gone were the smiles meant just for him.

"Are you sure she is gone?" Chimera stood beside him, staring at the lake, hands shoved in his pocket.

"Are you going to spout some bullshit about her spirit being all fucking around me?" Jett staggered to his feet. "Because that's a load of crap."

"The soul is something invented by the religious establishments to try and appease those who fear death. It's nonsense. Dead is dead."

"Do you think we'll ever find her body?" Because he hated to think of her in that cold watery grave forever.

"I know exactly where her body is. Would you like to see it?"

"Mother fucker. What have you done to her?" Jett lunged but was drunker than expected, given Chimera danced out of reach.

"Calm yourself. I don't have her. I said you could see her."

"How?"

"Follow me."

Chimera took him to his office, the public one that he kept on the ground level of the clinic. He opened a closet door and beckoned Jett.

Turned out it wasn't a closet but a slim elevator. It shot down, not too far by his reckoning, and opened onto a room he'd never even suspected existed. A room massive in size with a wall comprised of glass. Glass holding back tons of water.

"What the fuck is this?" he asked. "An aquarium?"

"Of a sort." Chimera approached the glass, hands tucked behind his back. "It's actually a view into the cavern that forms the lake.

The lake that took his Red. Jett stayed away from the glass wall, not sure if he could handle seeing her floating corpse.

Chimera kept talking. "Originally I had this built for my pleasure. I've always felt the ocean held so many of the world's secrets. But then it became practical. Early in my research, a few of my subjects treated with aquatic splices found themselves unable to tolerate living on land, but thrived in the water."

"You mean there really are monsters in the lake?" The dull edge of liquor still gripped him as Jett approached the window.

"I wouldn't call them monsters. Some are quite beautiful. A few days ago, we acquired a new addition." Chimera flicked a switch, illuminating the water from all directions. The clarity was startling. He could see myriad fish swimming around.

But that wasn't what held him riveted in place.

Swimming toward him, her red hair floating, the separate strands undulating, was Becky. Not dead after all. But also not quite the woman he'd left. For one, she appeared to be breathing water, and the skin of her body, arms and legs, shimmered, as if covered in scales. Only her face remained untouched, gorgeous.

Alive. She reached for him with a smile.

His eyes widened. "Holy shit." He palmed the glass and whispered, "She's a fucking mermaid."

Elation filled him, then confusion. "I don't understand." Only to suddenly grasp things with a clarity that roused his anger. "You did this to her!"

"Not me."

"Don't fucking lie. Those treatments you said you were giving her, they changed her." He advanced on the doctor, fists clenched.

"While my treatments might have eased the process, it wasn't that which transformed Nurse Hendrickson but the vials she stole and used."

"What?" The accusation stopped him in his tracks.

"You heard me. Your paramour stole from me and then foolishly injected herself." Chimera turned to the glass. "She should have died. All the others did, and yet look at her. A mermaid sans tail."

"Can you fix her?"

"Perhaps," Chimera mused. "But I'd need to have access to her. I'll require samples, which I can't acquire while she's in the lake."

"Then how do we get her out?" He approached the glass, still trying to process the fact that she floated on the other side.

"That is why I fetched you. We need your help to get her out of there."

Jett lifted his hand to the glass. "Tell me what I have to do."

CHAPTER NINETEEN

It took Becky awhile before she stopped huddling on the bottom of the lake. The big fish who'd brought here to the underwater cave had left.

Left her alone. In the dark.

Despite being in the water, she didn't feel cold. Although, when a school of fish passed and left behind a warm spot...let's just say she changed places.

Breathing didn't hurt. Not anymore. She could suck in great big lungfuls of water with ease. As to how she didn't die?

It might have had to do with the fact that she'd changed. A fact she first noticed when some jerk threw a switch and turned on a light.

After hours of darkness, the illumination proved

jarring. She blinked and looked around her in shock. It was one thing to know she resided in some kind of watery cavern, another to see it. The rock walls all around were striated and smoothed by the water. The bottom, a pebbled and muddy mess. Left and right of her, fish swam, some in schools, others alone. All of them oblivious to the giant window.

A window overlooking an empty room. Not much in it, a pair of chairs facing the glass with a table between them. An observation chamber. But no one was in it. She learned the lights were on a timer. On for a few hours a day. Timed to come on at the same time as several openings in the wall squirted something into the water.

She wrinkled her nose at the taste it left behind. Poison wouldn't leave her feeling more energized and clear-headed. Some kind of nutrient addition. Just like the shellfish that were propelled out of a hole above were food.

That first time the chute opened, she ignored the raining shrimp. The fact that she craved some of the little fish swimming by wasn't something she wanted to contemplate. She'd never been big on the whole sushi thing. At all!

The second day, when that light came on and it rained chunks of tuna, her hungry belly didn't care if it was raw.

By the fourth day, she was one of the first to grab a handful. Better than scrounging like some of the other creatures that lurked from under rocks and shallow caves.

Things that made her shudder—*Because I think they were once human like me.*

Once being the key word. Becky wasn't herself anymore.

Becky had become a mermaid, which was kind of weird. While many little girls dreamed of being a mermaid, she wasn't one of them. She didn't think the scales adorning her skin were pretty. Their iridescent sheen only served to remind her she'd done this to herself.

Why didn't I pay more attention to the monster in his lab?

The only saving grace was she retained her human shape and face. She'd seen her reflection in the glass. Her two legs. Two arms. Still two boobs. Barely hidden by the shirt that billowed around her every time she moved.

No tail, thank goodness. Still, she'd become something other than human, which was quite scary. Not to mention lonely. The other fish in the lake? They didn't talk much. But at least she could see them, her eyesight clear despite looking at everything through water.

Funny how in some respects she was part fish, able to breathe, scales shimmering on her arms, eyes with a strange film to protect them. Yet in others, she wasn't. Not a single fin to be seen. A hybrid mermaid who really wished she'd not played with Chimera's potions.

But at the same time...the pain in her lungs was gone. She was alive.

She just didn't know if it would last. Not to mention there were things in the lake. Scary things. None of them had tried to eat her yet, but she did worry. She'd seen the bones lying at the bottom. One appeared to be a human skull.

If only she could figure out how to escape. She feared leaving the room with the light and the food. What if she left the cavern and never found it again?

On the fifth day, the light came on as usual, but there was a difference. A man stood looking out the window. Dr. Chimera, whose eyes widened upon seeing her.

Then he smiled.

A smile that didn't say, *Don't worry, Becky, I can fix this*, but rather the kind of grin a shark might give before making you its lunch.

The light turned off abruptly, leaving her in shocking darkness.

Her heart pounded.

What did it mean?

The illumination only lasted a few minutes, not the usual hours. The food still dropped from above. She could sense more than see it falling around her, yet she didn't grab for any.

Why did Chimera turn off the light?

Had he gone to get help? If that were the case, then why not leave the illumination?

She sank to the bottom and pondered the possible reasons. None made any sense. When the lights returned suddenly, she perked up. Especially since she saw Chimera back at the window.

And he wasn't alone.

She saw another shape with him.

Jett!

She swam toward him, a bright smile on her lips. She pressed her hands against the glass.

He stared in shock.

She blew him a kiss and then giggled, which had the effect of making bubbles. Hopefully he realized she didn't fart.

When the water cleared, he was yelling at Chimera. Waving his arms, pointing at her.

She couldn't hear what he said but could imagine it involved a lot of F bombs. But if anyone could save her, it was Jett.

When he was done yelling at Chimera, he

returned to the glass and palmed it. She placed her hand so that it fit against his. So close and yet so far apart.

Jett mouthed something at her.

She cocked her head and shrugged.

He spoke again, his lips moving more slowly. When that didn't work, he pointed.

She shook her head and lifted her hands.

He scowled for a moment, and then he left.

The lights were still on, but it felt dark. She bobbed sadly, wondering if he'd finally given up on her.

Only Jett returned, holding a sheet of paper and a pen. He spent a second scribbling and then flipped it over to show her.

"Meet me. Lake's edge."

Easy enough if she knew where it was. She frowned then traced letters on the glass.

Lost.

He frowned and turned to the doctor, gestured a few times, probably swore a few more before using the pen and paper again.

Hold on.

Uh, okay. Because she totally had other places to go.

Jett left again, this time with Chimera. They were gone awhile. Only Chimera returned. He wrote a message.

Go to ceiling. Fish food.

She frowned at first then beamed. Of course, there must be access to the cavern via the food slots.

Duh. Why hadn't she thought of that! She clapped her hands underwater, which didn't make a sound and, given the resistance of water, barely made an impression. She waggled her butt as she swam upward, not at all graceful like a mermaid, more like a wiggling worm pulling herself awkwardly through molasses, but at least she had buoyance to help her, and she made it to the trap door.

Which was closed.

So she knocked. *Tap. Tap.*

There was no sound when the hinge released, and she almost got bonked. She darted to the side as it swung open. Then stared up the hole, the light in the cavern not illuminating it.

It seemed big enough, if you didn't mind coffin-sized spaces.

Indecision had her hovering. Then a light shone down.

Someone was at the top of the feeding chute.

Taking in a deep mouthful of water, she arrowed into the tunnel, needing her hands to pull her up since it proved too narrow to swim.

She floated to the surface, aiming for the beam of light, and emerged into the air, only to gasp.

Choke. Her lungs spasmed.

She fell back under the water, scared and frustrated.

It didn't help that she saw Jett overhead, leaning over the chute's opening.

She tried again, popping her head above the surface, the air hitting her skin. She opened her mouth and gargled.

She felt back under, utterly dejected. Jett remained overheard, his usually grim expression creased in concern.

The only good news was, without the glass separating them, she could hear him, but given it filtered through water, it was a little garbled.

"Gonna find a way to fix this."

How could he fix this? Other than filleting, breading, and frying her in lard, what could he do to make her better?

He held out his hand to her, the one thing she could stick out of the water without discomfort. She clasped his fingers tight.

"Chimera says he can help."

Help the same way he'd helped Larry and the minotaur guy?

She shook her head, trying to speak, but the

sound emerged odd and discordant. A series of whistles and high-pitched noises.

I sound like a dolphin.

But Jett didn't run away in horror from his aquatic girlfriend.

Nope. He pulled a gun and shot her!

CHAPTER TWENTY

As soon as Jett shot Becky, he had to move fast. The sedative worked immediately, and she slumped. Good thing he'd grabbed her hand ahead of time. He yanked her free of the chute, hating this part of the plan, yet what choice did he have? Her slick and slim body emerged easily, but she immediately began to choke.

With her soaking body secured in his arms, Jett ran past the machinery. Past the metal wheels and pipes, all part of Chimera's elaborate natural aquarium. Hearing her gasping for breath, the adrenaline coursed, moving him faster.

No one stupidly got in his way. Good thing. He would have bowled them over and trampled them in his race to get her to the tank in Chimera's second hidden lab.

The plan had been hastily hatched with his boss. He just wished he could have explained to Red what he would do. He'd seen the wide-eyed look of betrayal in her eyes when he shot her, but he had no choice. He'd seen her despair when she couldn't breathe outside of the water. Worse, he feared she'd flee. Then how would he find her?

Chimera said he could fix her, and while Jett didn't always trust the bastard, he wanted to believe he told the truth. If he didn't, Jett wouldn't hesitate to put a bullet between his eyes.

When and how this woman became so important was beyond him. A killer shouldn't care. Yet somehow, he'd begun to care too fucking much, which meant he wasn't about to let her go without a fight.

The maintenance door opened at his approach, Chimera obviously watching, and he put on a burst of speed as her breathing stuttered. Halted. Her skin was clammy cold.

He ran through a hall inset with porthole windows to Chimera's other lab. The door to it open wide, the doctor standing in it, beckoning.

"Hurry. She won't last much longer outside of water. The tank is ready for her." The doctor swept an arm to show him.

Jett sprinted past and saw the big vat, the liquid clear, bubbles rising from the bottom.

He leaned over the edge and slipped her in. She sank, and for a moment, he wanted to reach in and grab her. Pull her to him and hold her tight. Wanted to apologize and yet he couldn't have said for what. Somehow, he'd failed her. Made her think she had to take that serum.

How desperate she must have been to inject herself. But so long as she lived, they could do something about her situation. He could learn to scuba dive. Maybe get her a water tank for breathing.

Something...

Chimera stood beside him, staring at her lifeless body. "Good job."

"Don't patronize me. This is my fault. I should have realized something was wrong." Not left when she clung to him tightly and whispered goodbye.

"My fault, too. I should have told her I was treating her."

At least the sudden injections of the serum hadn't killed her. Which seemed kind of odd. Usually the more drastic changes happened over the course of time. Never all at once. "When do we start reversing the mermaid effect?"

"Why would we do that? She's perfect," Chimera said, sounding pleased with himself.

Jett shot him a look. "Perfect? Are you fucking

kidding me? She's in a tank of water because she can't breathe."

"On the contrary, she's breathing perfectly fine."

"Underwater," he said through gritted teeth.

"Do you know she's the first successful mermaid we've created? The others..." Chimera trailed off. "Let's just say they didn't succeed."

"You didn't create her. She did this by accident."

"Not entirely."

"What's that supposed to mean?" Jett growled.

"You asked me to treat her cancer. I'm sure tests will show her completely free of tumors."

"So this is a side effect?"

"No, it's quite intentional." Chimera turned from the tank, hands tucked behind him. "As a matter of fact, she is exactly what the client wants. It just took us longer than expected. Who knew the sudden addition of serum would initiate the change and so rapidly. This is fabulous news. It could be we've been going about the treatment all wrong."

"Rewind to the part where you said she's what a client wants."

"Did you know there's a market demand for a mermaid? Mind you, we had to lower the price given the fact she has two legs instead of a tail, but she will still fetch a fine figure."

"You're planning to sell her!" he blurted out. The shock had him gaping.

"Yes. Not our usual thing, I will admit. Most people want the treatment, not the test subject result. But in this case, the client has a particular fetish. He's quite the scuba diver and snorkeler enthusiast. Don't worry. He's got a private lake that he's had equipped with an underwater palace fit for a mermaid princess."

"You can't be fucking serious. She's not a whore for you to sell."

"Then what do you suggest I do?" Chimera turned a cold stare on him. "I can't set her free. She knows too much. Not to mention she took something she shouldn't have. Should we kill her?"

"No." The word burst out of him. "Give her to me."

"Give her to you?" Chimera chuckled. "Now you're just being foolish. I know you've had some fun with her, but she's a woman, like any other."

Actually, she wasn't. "I'll buy her."

"You don't have enough money. And besides, where would you keep her? How?"

"You can't do this."

"Can't? Actually, I can do whatever I like." Chimera's tone turned cold. "Or have you forgotten who you're talking to?"

"Being able to do something doesn't mean you should. Selling her, it's wrong." Never mind the fact he wouldn't have said a word if it were anyone else but Red.

"Don't tell me you've grown a conscience and feelings at this point of the game."

Yes. But admitting it aloud wouldn't serve him well. "Of course not."

"Good. Because I'd hate to have to change our working arrangement." And by change, he knew Chimera meant a sedative and a trip to the basement to become part of the project group.

There was no quitting Chimaeram Clinic. He should know since he often was the one who dealt with those who had a change of heart. So what did that leave?

He could kill Chimera right now. Bare hands around his throat. Take him to the ground and stomp on his chest until he crushed his heart.

But killing Chimera wouldn't fix Becky. It wouldn't give Jett a chance to make other plans. To figure out a way to save her.

He needed more time.

"You're the boss. You want to sell her, then that's your business."

"Glad to hear it because, for the next little while, your only task is to guard the mermaid until we can make arrangements to have her moved into the client's possession."

"How long until that happens?"

"Given the buyer's eagerness? A few days at the most."

Which didn't buy Jett much time. Doubtful a cure could be found that quickly. But he'd toss her back in the lake before he let Chimera sell her.

Don't worry, Red. I won't let anyone take you.

CHAPTER TWENTY-ONE

WHAT A STRANGE DREAM. BECKY IMAGINED she'd turned into a mermaid and was stuck in a lake. Then Jett came along, but instead of saving her, he shot her!

So silly. She rolled over and hit something hard. Come to think of it, under her was hard too.

What happened to my bed?

Her eyes fluttered open underwater, and she stared. Mostly because she didn't dare blink.

In that moment, she realized it wasn't a dream. Her nightmare had come true. *I'm a fish.*

And Jett had tranquilized her. But perhaps not for nefarious reason.

The lake was gone, and she appeared to be in some kind of tank. A large one, but it didn't take long for her to realize it was a prison. Glass surrounded her on three sides, the fourth appeared to be a solid wall—that could have used a landscape image. Didn't all aquariums have one?

From the bottom of the tank, in two of the corners, bubbles rose to the surface and popped. She shoved herself away from the bottom and discovered she could surface.

Like a fish out of water, she gasped and choked when she popped her head into the air that acted as an impenetrable buffer between her and the ladder out of this tank.

Returning to the water, she glared at the freedom that mocked her. There was no point in putting a lid on the tank since she couldn't leave the water.

Pressing her hands on the glass front, she focused outward. Computers with monitors displaying stats on a long counter. Stats about her she'd wager. An island with beakers and vials. More medical equipment. She found herself in a lab. A research lab with her as the rat in a cage.

She'd exchange one sentence for another.

I only wanted to live.

A red blink caught her attention, and she glanced upward to find a camera watching. Spying on her.

Rage filled her at yet another sign that she had

lost her freedom. But this at least she could do something about.

She dipped down then shot up, flinging water at the camera again and again until she heard a sizzle and the light went out with a pop. The faint line of smoke made her smile.

Not for long. Depressed and unable to find a happy spin on things, she sank to the bottom.

Motion from the corner of her eye brought her attention to the man entering the lab.

Jett. Looking as fierce as ever.

He approached the glass and pressed his hand against it. For a moment, she was tempted to greet him as well. Almost accepted the apology in his face.

But he'd shot her.

Shot. Me.

She turned her back on him.

"Don't do that." She could hear him despite the glass. "I thought I was helping you."

The snort emerged as a series of bubbles.

"I had to get you out of there. There're things in that lake. Bad things..."

She whirled in the water, her hair swirling around her in a cloud. The fabric of her shirt clung and billowed at the same time, but she might as well have been naked since it did nothing to hide her form.

Since she couldn't reply, she scowled and shook her head before crossing her arms.

"I get it you're pissed. And not just because I tranqed you. I should have been there for you."

His being around wouldn't have changed the outcome. She would have taken the serum no matter what.

"I know the situation doesn't seem good. And you're right. It's not. Fucking Chimera lied to me."

She arched a brow.

"Yeah, I shouldn't be surprised. But..." He looked so downcast, his shoulders slumped. "I had to do something to help you. I couldn't let you live like this."

Being a mermaid wasn't ideal by any means. But so long as she lived, she had a chance.

"I should have left you in that lake until I had a better plan. Fuck, I still might put you back there rather than let Chimera go through with his plan to sell you."

Her mouth opened into a round O. The word "What?" emerged as bubbles and noise.

"He thinks I'm okay with his plan." His expression darkened. "Like fuck am I letting him sell you off. I'll shoot him first."

For some reason that made her smile. Becky approached the glass and touched it. His hand met hers. Glass might separate them, but she still felt the same about him, and it seemed he cared, too.

"I don't know what to do." He scrubbed hand over his bristled jaw. "I don't know where to go. But I promise, I won't let anyone take you, Red."

She tapped the glass and rose to the surface. Grabbed hold of the lip and hoisted herself out of the water. The air in the lab hit her wet skin, and she gasped. But she didn't sink back immediately. She held her breath.

Jett climbed the stairs on the side of the tank and faced her.

"Jeezus, Red. What a mess we're in."

She liked the use of we. She beckoned him closer. He drew near, near enough that she could press her mouth to his. Cold lips meeting hot ones. A kiss to remind them both she was alive. And so long as she lived, there was a chance. A chance to get out of this mess.

He broke the kiss first. "Get back under there before you pass out from lack of air," he admonished.

She popped down, a quick inhale, and then up again, demanding another kiss. And he was weak. Weak when it came to her, which made her strong.

There had to be a way they could still be together.

Up and down she went, a quick breath of water, then up for another kiss.

Again. And again. Until he finally groaned.

"Enough."

She popped under water and cocked her head, mouthing, "Why?"

"Because I want you."

She spread her arms in invitation.

Frustration marred his expression. "If only we could. But it's impossible."

A lifted brow was her reply.

"Fuck it."

He stripped, his clothes hitting the floor, until he was naked, but he didn't join her right away. First, he grabbed a stool. He slid it in the tank before getting in with her.

She wondered at it until he stood on it, the height enough to keep his head above water without having to swim.

But a fascinating prospect for her since that made his body so accessible.

He grabbed hold of her and brought her close for a skin-to-skin kiss. Sinking under water partway through it, his mouth meshed with hers, his skin scorching against her chillier flesh.

But she wanted more than a kiss. She braced her hands on his shoulders, and with only her lips, she traced the edge of his unshaven jaw, nipping it lightly with her teeth. She then followed the strong column of his neck, tracing a path down it to his pecs. His well-defined pectorals with his hard nipples.

She knew from experience how sensitive they were, so she spent a moment playing with them while he did his best not to tremble.

But he did finally move when she bit, bringing forth a bubbly laugh. Floating around his midsection, she glanced upward and saw him staring. How fierce he looked, and yet, at the same time, she finally recognized that look in his eyes.

He loves me.

He might not have said it, but it was there in his touch, his expression, in the things he did just to be with her.

The urge to kiss him almost overwhelmed. Instead, she settled for dragging her nails over his flesh, scraping his nipples.

Then lower. Teasing her way down his body over the flat tautness of his belly. She had to grab hold of his thighs to anchor herself. Odd how, when she was awake, she floated.

With her lips in the right spot, she brushed the tip of his cock. Felt the rigid steel of him, the pulse of his arousal. She opened wide and took him into her mouth. Took as much as she could and sucked. Which was a different sensation than with air. She could blow while she suctioned, the force of expelled bubbles tickling his dick.

His hips jerked. She held on tight. Sucked some more, sliding her lips down his thick length. Then up again. Back and forth.

Her body floated, which made it easy for him to grab hold and turn her. Turn her so she was upside down in the water.

But she didn't mind because as she devoured him, he lifted her bottom half free of the water, enough he could latch his mouth onto her sex.

So this was how mermaids 69ed.

She loved it.

Loved him.

Sucked him. Bobbed up and down on his cock while also kneading his sac, squeezing and releasing.

He toyed with her sex, doing his best to distract. His tongue probing between her lips. His lips nuzzling at her clit. When she cried out, the sound vibrated the shaft in her mouth. He groaned in returned as he tongued her.

And she almost came. He sensed it, and next thing she knew, he was twisting her in the water again, flipping her so her ass was against his belly and she faced away from him. She floated horizontally, her legs spread around his waist. He still stood on the stool, head above water to breathe, but she remained under. Easy to move. Easy for him to grab hold and press the tip of his shaft against her lower lips.

He impaled her, seating the full length of his cock inside her channel, stretching her. Hands on her hips, he controlled the pace. Pulled her back and forth, thrusting firmly, claiming her. Finding a way despite their differences.

He drove deeper. Faster. Faster.

A sound emerged from her, a high note of pleasure that thrummed through the water. And his pace quickened, the thrusts fast and hard. Each deep ram hitting her G-spot, pushing her closer to the edge. Closer.

She flipped on him so she floated on her back, legs wrapped around his hips. He kept the rhythm going, filling her. Staring at her, mouthing something she couldn't hear through the slosh of waves.

Her orgasm hit her hard. A ripple stronger than any tide. More pleasurable than she could have imagined. Her sex fisted him tight, and she keened, an odd ululating sound that filled the water with a hum. He thrust one last time into her, and she felt the hot spurt as he came.

Came and didn't leave. He dragged her close to

him, her head tucked against his chest under water, his hand stroking her hair.

Whispering, "I'll find a way to save you, Red."

She doubted he could. But she would treasure the sentiment. She wasn't one to cling to false hope.

When he exited the tank, she watched him. Watched with melancholy as he dressed, realizing this would probably be the last time they were together.

After all, where could they go? How would they get there? The best she could hope for was to escape into the lake. But Jett couldn't join her.

Nor should he. He deserved a normal life. She loved him too much to want anything else.

He'd no sooner finished dressing than the door opened and Chimera sauntered in. She rushed the glass, palms pressed against it, and hissed, the sound more a harsh stream of bubbles than anything.

"Are you done playing with the merchandise?"

"How long have you been out there?" Jett snapped.

"Long enough. A good thing I didn't promise the client a virgin. If you're done screwing the package, the chopper is waiting."

"So soon? I thought you said a few days."

"And I thought you said you didn't care,"

Chimera taunted. He stepped past Jett. "You, my dear, are about to make someone very, very happy."

She cast a panicked look at Jett.

Was this the end? She palmed the glass, pleading with her gaze.

Don't let him take me.

Her dark hero raised a gun.

CHAPTER TWENTY-TWO

A MAN COULD BE SURE ABOUT ONE THING WHEN he pulled a weapon on his boss. *I'll need to find a new job.* Which was fine because Jett wasn't about to let Chimera sell or take Becky from him. Not now. Not fucking ever. If he had to shoot this fucker to free her, he'd do it and sleep like a baby after.

As to how he'd manage to support them? He had some money socked away. Plenty of it, given the clinic didn't require much spending. Enough to buy a house with an indoor pool or a place by a lake. Anything to keep Becky safe.

"You aren't taking her anywhere," Jett growled.

The doctor turned around and arched a brow at the sight of the gun. "Giving orders now? Put that thing down. You're not going to shoot me over a woman."

Not just a woman. His Red. The one person that made him feel.

His aim didn't waver. "I will shoot and not lose sleep over it."

"Shoot me, then what? You won't get far. Once I wake up..." Chimera let the threat linger rather than state it.

Pity Chimera knew the difference between a real gun and the tranquilizing kind. What he didn't grasp was Jett didn't need a bullet to kill him. "I'm going to make this real simple for you. If you want to live, then you'll let Becky go."

"Go where?" Chimera sneered. "Going to bring her to your room and stick her in the shower?"

"Sure as hell beats you selling her off to some pervert."

"And here I thought I could trust you. That you understood my vision." Chimera shook his head, hands tucked behind his back.

"I don't give a shit about your secrets. Nor do I give a rat's ass about your so-called vision. But you should have left Becky alone."

"You never gave a damn about the other nurses I played with."

"You're right. I didn't." But he'd not fallen for those women. Just Red.

"I'm going to give you one last chance to walk

away. Go to your room and report to me in the morning. We'll pretend this never happened."

Walking away wasn't an option, and Chimera obviously wouldn't budge.

Jett fired.

The dart flew straight and true.

And missed!

Chimera moved. Moved faster than should have been possible. And more astonishing, pulled a gun.

A real gun.

Ah, shit.

It was Jett's turn to move, running toward Chimera, ducking on instinct, hearing the bullet as it whizzed past his ear.

Too close.

Jett dove at the doctor before he could fire again. Grabbed the arm with the gun and held it aloft while he grappled.

Chimera might possess a slim build and give off a nerdy vibe, but it turned out the man was strong. He more than matched Jett in strength, and they grappled, grunting and straining as they sought to best each other.

Jett thought he had the upper hand until Chimera snarled, the sound low and raspy. "Enough already." The man's eyes glowed golden, and his lip pulled back in a snarl that proved less than human.

In that moment Chimera got stronger.

Much stronger.

Jett found himself on the defensive, getting pushed around. A slick spot on the floor caught his foot, sweeping it out from under him. It threw him off balance, which, in turn, caused Chimera to stumble. They both hit the ground hard. So hard Jett lost his grip on the gun arm.

The doctor's hand hit the floor. His finger must have spasmed. The firearm went off.

Bang.

The bullet hit the front of the tank, sank right into the thick glass in front of Red's wide eyes.

For a moment, Jett thought they'd gotten lucky, and then the point of impact splintered. Spider-webbed into a handful of cracks then a dozen, the lines zipping across the surface, honeycombing the glass.

The groan of water against compromised walls was the only warning before it burst. Gallons and gallons of water gushed out in a torrent. Flooding the room. Ruining equipment.

As if he cared. His only concern was the woman who came tumbling out.

"Oh shit, Red!" He shouted for her as he ran across the floor, slipping and sliding. Landing on his knees in a skid and dragging her into his lap.

Her mouth opened and shut as she gasped for air. The fright in her eyes matched that squeezing his heart.

"Hold on, Red. I'll get you to the lake." If he ran, he could make it.

He stood with her in his arms and turned to find Chimera, blood pouring down his temple, standing in front of the door, the gun once more aimed at Jett.

"Are you fucking kidding me?" The black-eyed bole of the gun wasn't about to stop him. "Move, asshole."

"I think not. You've disappointed me, Jett. I thought you were a company man."

"I told you not to hurt her."

"Betraying me because of your feelings for a girl?" Chimera shook his head. "What did I tell you about caring for them?"

The same thing Jett's father had told him. Didn't matter. Maybe this thing with Red would fizzle. Or she'd stomp on his heart. But only a coward would refuse to even try.

"I'm leaving with her." He had to because if she didn't get to water, she'd die. Already, she trembled in his arms, her mouth opening and shutting. Her eyes pleading for help.

"I think it's time for a lesson. Time for you to remember who gives the orders." Chimera didn't shout; he didn't have to. His voice carried far enough to be heard. "Aqua lab lockdown."

Jett didn't have to hear the whirring and clicks of locks engaging to realize they were fucked. Those doors wouldn't open unless Chimera ordered them to. Which meant he couldn't kill the guy. But he also didn't have time to waste.

Red's breathing grew more ragged.

"What happened to be being giddy about your first ever mermaid?" Jett argued. "Are you seriously telling me you'd rather see her die?"

"Me?" Chimera had the temerity to inject a query with shock. "Don't blame me for this. She is the one who stole my serum. And you're the one who refused to do your duty. If her death is anyone's fault, it's yours."

"You sick motherfucker."

"Don't talk to me about my mother. A mother doesn't abandon her crippled child," spat Chimera.

Which explained a lot. Becky convulsed in his arms, bubbles and water wretched from her lips. Her eyes rolled back. The gasps stopped. She went rigid. Then still.

So very still.

Jett's head bowed. He closed his eyes for a moment and allowed himself one deep breath—a shuddering one that threatened to overwhelm—before he knelt to lay her gently on the floor.

There were no tears in him. Nothing but a cold empty place. Only one thing could warm him now.

He lifted his head and growled. "You did this."

"No, you—"

The doctor never finished his sentence because Jett charged, ignoring the bullet that ripped through the flesh of his shoulder, ignoring everything but his need to kill the man who'd taken the one good thing in his life. The one person he cared about.

He hit Chimera and slammed him into the door. He managed to rap his head a few times, enough to daze the other man before wrapping his hands around his neck.

Squeezing.

"I'm going to kill you. Fucking bastard. Fucking —" His voice broke as he cursed Chimera. Broke and choked with the tears he couldn't release.

Chimera didn't look so cocky now with his eyes bulging. And Jett would have killed him, killed him because he deserved it, if he'd not heard a faint, "Don't."

CHAPTER TWENTY-THREE

BECKY WASN'T DEAD.

She knew this because she was pretty sure dead people didn't breathe.

She sat up and blinked. Took in a deep lungful of air. Air, not water. A glance at her skin showed the scales fading, as if absorbed back into her flesh.

Becky stood on wobbly legs—feeling much like a sailor stepping ashore after a long stay at sea. The world seemed sharper without a watery haze covering it. Colder, too. Air kissed her damp skin, and she shivered.

Better shivering than in a tank.

Noticing Jett hard at work choking the life out of Chimera, she felt a need to step in. Not out of any compassion for the man. However, given her situation, it didn't seem prudent to kill the one person who might be able to reverse what she'd done to herself. Also, the one person who could release them from this locked room.

Still, there was a temptation to let Jett kill the doctor. Kill a man who so obviously played with things he shouldn't.

He isn't God. However, Chimera was brilliant. Brilliant enough that perhaps she might not have to die after all.

"Don't." Her voice emerged rusty. Soft. Barely a whisper in a room that hummed with machinery.

For a moment, she thought Jett wouldn't listen. Then he turned a haunted expression on her.

"Red? Are you okay?"

Loaded question. But in this case, there was only one reply for Jett. She nodded. "I think so. I can breathe." And breathe deeply without pain. Did this mean the cancer was gone?

Releasing Chimera, Jett launched himself at her and scooped her in his arms, hugging her tight. "Jeezus fucking Christ, I thought I'd lost you."

"Still might if you don't ease up, big guy." A laughing rebuke that she didn't actually mean. Let him squeeze her. She was happy to be alive.

The hug eased, but he kept her close. "How do you feel?"

"Pretty damned good actually."

"Are your lungs hurting?"

She shook her head. "Not at the moment."

"That is fucking great," Jett exclaimed.

"It doesn't mean she's healed. We should x-ray her."

Jett turned a dark glare on Chimera. "Don't you fucking come near her."

"Someone needs to examine her." The doctor had regained his composure.

"It won't be you." The snarled words sounded so sexy.

"Are you really going to let our little spat stand in the way of her best interests?"

"Spat?" Jett laughed, the sound full of incredulity. "You tried to kill us."

"No, I threatened you. You didn't back down."

"Because you were going to sell her, asshole!"

Chimera shrugged. "It was business, not personal."

"It was fucking personal to me."

"Obviously I miscalculated your affection for the woman. Would you feel better if I cancelled the sale?"

"I'd feel better if I'd finished choking you." Jett bristled. Only her soft hand on his bicep stemmed him from doing anything rash.

"Don't. He's screwing with you. He is obviously

not going to sell me because now I'm too valuable. Aren't I?" She smirked at Chimera. "You want to know how come I can breathe air again." She'd seen the surprise on his face, the curiosity. And truth be told, she wanted to know what it meant, too.

"What do you say we come to an arrangement?" Chimera offered.

"I am not making a deal with you." Jett's firm reply held no room for negotiation.

However, truth was, Chimera, slimy as he might be, remained her best chance of beating whatever ailed her. Already she'd gone from dying to...who knew what the future held? "What are you thinking?" she asked.

"You can't be serious," Jett barked. "The guy just tried to kill us."

"And none of this would have happened if I'd not stolen the serum from his lab. So I'd say we're even." She turned her gaze on Chimera. "What are you proposing?"

"A truce first of all. No killing by any of us." The doctor cast Jett a look that was returned with a grim scowl. "I want to examine you, Becky. Let us see what happened to those tumors. Run some tests. Conduct some MRIs and ultrasounds. Blood samples. Urine."

"And how long will that take?" Jett asked.

"Awhile," Becky replied for Chimera. "Given the unusual circumstances, I imagine he'll want to monitor me closely for some time."

"Correct."

"You expect us to stay here so you can study her?" Jett's lips curled. "Do I look fucking stupid? You want to make her a prisoner."

"Not a prisoner, but we do need to monitor her situation because, let's be honest here, we don't know exactly how the treatment has affected her. Is the cancer truly gone? Will it return? Does she only require air to breath, or will she revert once more into an aquatic state? What of other side effects?"

"What side effects?" Jett barked.

Chimera shrugged. "That's just it. I don't know. She's something new. Wonderful and unique."

"She is also not for sale."

Chimera spread his hands. "Would it help if I said that was a bad idea?"

"Do you think?" Jett's sarcasm ran deep.

"How do we know you're not just saying this? That you're not just looking for another chance to ship me off?" Becky played devil's advocate for Jett's benefit.

"Because I'm not the devil you think I am. Yes, my agreeing to sell you was in poor taste." Jett growled. Chimera amended. "Very poor taste. But would it help if I said you were worth ten million dollars?"

Her eyes widened. "That much?"

Jett's gaze narrowed. "That is a lot of money to give up."

"But even more to gain now," Chimera explained. "A mermaid is an oddity with very little practical use. But someone who can breathe water or air..." His face lit with excitement. "Can you imagine the market for such a thing?"

She could. The applications to not only aquatic activities but off planet, in places where air might not be in plentiful supply. If Chimera could manipulate lungs to adapt to any condition...he was right. It would be epic. Revolutionary medicine worth more than ten million, or even ten billion, dollars.

And she might be the start of it.

"I don't know if I want Red being your personal guinea pig." Jett's arms crossed, and he glared.

Adorable.

"You'd be here to keep an eye. Paid of course. Can't have anyone stealing the world's first mermaid."

"I am not going to live like those patients. Locked away or kept in a coma," Becky added.

Chimera waved a hand. "Those are difficult cases, completely different from you. I see us more as partners. Yes, you'll have to do some tests and give some blood, but I want you to keep on working as my assistant. Discover with me."

The temptation dangled. Better than any carrot.

"I don't believe you. I tried to kill you," Jett said flatly.

"You're not the first. But I'm not a man to hold a grudge."

Becky wasn't entirely sure she believed that; however, she did know that Chimera valued one thing above all others. Discovery. And with Jett by her side, she wanted to be a part of it.

"Do we have a deal or not?" Chimera asked.

For her, there was only one answer. "I'll stay. But on a few conditions. One, Jet and I get the biggest set of rooms you've got."

"Done. I have a suite just vacated by Dr. Jackal, who moved to our European division."

"I'm not done. The second thing I want is the exclusive scoop when the clinic goes public."

"That might not be for years," Chimera warned.

Years...not something she thought she'd get many of. Now, she might get a lifetime.

With the man she loved.

When the deal was hammered out, Chimera released the locks on the door. Not that Jett trusted him. The portal slid open, and he said, "After you."

"Such suspicion," Chimera grumbled, stepping through. Jett followed next before he allowed her to join them in the hall.

No soldiers waited to greet them.

And the suite they were assigned was bigger and nicer than any apartment she'd ever lived in.

The bed a true king-sized with fresh sheets.

But first, a shower. Not just because she needed to cleanse herself but because her body craved the moisture. She might be breathing air again, and yet the core of her remained changed.

Jett didn't seem to care. He laid the gun he'd filched from the aqua lab on the counter, suspicion keeping him tense.

Watchful.

"Aren't you going to join me?" she asked, letting the warm spray run down over her body, leaving it slick and glistening.

"I don't trust that bastard," he growled.

She turned her face into the warm shower, eyes closed, enjoying the clear freshness of it, the heat. "I don't either. But there is no other choice." No other doctor could help with her condition. No one else in the world could help keep the cancer at bay and give her more time with this man.

"We can still escape. There are ways."

And live a life on the run? Always looking over

her shoulder. Wondering if the serum she'd taken would one day fail.

"I want to stay." She pivoted and leaned her back on the shower, offering a sultry gaze to him as she ran her fingers down the length of her torso. Teasing her own skin while remembering the touch of his fingers. The heat of his mouth and the tease of his tongue.

A pulse started between her legs. A hunger for the man who stared at her.

And only stared.

It seemed only right to give him a show. Grabbing the soap, she rubbed it between her palms, creating a frothy lather. She stroked those soapy fingers over her skin, sliding them with sensual languor over her already sensitized body, holding his gaze the entire time. Getting slicker between her legs the more his eyes smoldered.

She cupped her breasts, squeezed them. Rolled the nipples between her fingers. Saw him swallow when she said, "Are you sure you don't want to join me?"

"I need..." He couldn't finish the sentence. A war raged inside him, one that demanded he remained responsible and stand guard, while another part of him obviously longed to touch her.

So she made it even harder—his decision and his cock—by sliding a hand between her thighs. Slicks fingers slid across a clit already swollen and sensitive. She gently rubbed it, back and forth, her hips twitching with each pass.

Jett uttered a noise, a groan of surrender, and then he stripped before joining her finally, his naked body big and beautiful, pinning her to the wall.

"You drive me crazy," he said in between hot kisses.

Whereas for Becky. "You make me feel safe." Protected. Cherished.

And yes, worshipped when he dropped to his knees before her.

She ran fingers through his slick hair as he parted her thighs and then nudged one with a shoulder, getting her to lift it over him. Exposing her that he might lash his tongue against her swollen button. An electric current of desire thrummed through her, and she gasped. Trembled. Grabbed him by the hair, fingers digging in as she bucked.

He snared hold of her hips and held her steady. Held her that he might lick her, sliding his tongue back and forth across her sex, slipping it between her lips, stabbing deeper.

The pleasure engulfed. Made her feel alive. Warm. Feverish even as she leaned against the cold tile of the shower wall. Soft moans and gasps escaped her lips as he licked her and stroked her. She uttered a sharp cry when his lips caught and pulled at her clit.

Her body tensed and coiled. Her orgasm hovered. A wave pulled back from shore, waiting to crash.

But he didn't let her come on his tongue. He stood, the bigness of his body shadowing her. His lips caught hers, a fiery kiss where she could taste herself.

His hand slid between their bodies to finger her sex. Whereas she grabbed hold of his cock, feeling the velvety strength. The firmness. The pulse as he throbbed. Eager and ready.

She lifted a leg around his hip, an invitation he understood. The tip of his shaft penetrated, pushing and stretching. Filling her. Filling her deeply. Giving her something to clench.

Together, they rocked in rhythm, a grinding and rubbing motion that stimulated all the right places, had her squeezing him tight.

And when he came in hot splashing spurts, she followed, the tsunami unleashed, her body rippling in waves, her orgasm wet. So very wet.

Satisfying, too, leaving her boneless in his arms. But she didn't have to fear falling with Jett. He swept her into his arms. Wrapped her in a big fluffy towel then carried her to the bedroom. She protested when he didn't immediately join her, but he returned a moment later, gun in hand. A sobering reminder that their life remained tenuous.

Yet, she didn't care. For the first time in a long while, she had hope. Felt alive.

Best of all, she had Jett. A man who held her close and whispered, "I love you."

EPILOGUE

Over the course of the next few weeks, Jett never lowered his guard. Nor did he go anywhere unarmed. Yet, Chimera remained true to his word—or as true as a mad scientist could be. He made no move to sell her. No one threatened them. Nor did they become prisoners.

The medical studies of her body fascinated as she learned of the changes happening within. The cancer was gone. Not a single trace of it remained. She'd never been healthier as a matter of fact. So what if she needed to submerge every few days? She was a mermaid-human hybrid. The first and only one of her kind.

I am the big scoop. As such, she wanted to learn everything she could. Took great interest in the changes of her body and cells. With practice, she learned how to switch between breathing water and air without the panic. Began to enjoy her cravings for raw fish. Even made friends with the creatures living in the lake.

Most of all, she loved life. Loved Jett. Even if he grumbled at her decision to remain at the clinic. Despite the clean bill of health, she preferred to stay. They were doing wondrous things here. Epic things. And Dr. Chimera had promised her the scoop of a life-time when he was ready to tell the world. She'd already begun writing the book. A book that would one day make her famous, not that she really cared about such a thing anymore. She had bigger things to concentrate on.

She pressed her hands to her stomach. The ultra-sound showed a pair of tadpoles in there, literally, but the doctors didn't seem concerned. After all, a mermaid was special. Her babies, of course, should be special, too.

Jett, her loving husband, who'd married her in a lovely ceremony on the shore of the lake, would guard his children like he guarded his mermaid. Or so he claimed once he picked himself off the floor.

And if Chimera and his associates ever tried to use her babies in a way she didn't like... If Jett couldn't kill them all, then there were always her new friends in the lake she could call on. They were so very hungry. Especially the thing with long arms and a hearty appetite for flesh.

Adrian Chimera played the ultrasound video again and smiled.

"You look awfully pleased with yourself," Cerberus said, entering his office.

"Can you blame me? We succeeded." Not only in creating their first true mermaid, but babies, too.

"I thought you had another father planned for her."

At the reminder, Adrian shrugged. "This is actually better. I never thought for a moment my stern guard would fall for her."

"Jett almost killed you."

"I'm not that easy to kill," Adrian reminded. "And things worked out in the end." Becky had chosen to stay, which meant he got to monitor every step of her changes and pregnancy.

"What of Luke and the other nurse? Have the hunters located them yet"

That brought a scowl. "No. Seems they managed to not only disable their trackers but they've completely hidden their trail."

But they'd be back. His projects, the ones his staff called his pets, always came back.

HE WATCHED FROM THE WOODS. BIDING HIS time. Doing his best to not forget.

I am... The name eluded him for a moment. Who he was was a thing of the past. An almost forgotten memory.

I am Marcus.

But at the same time, he wasn't. And as he watched, he saw one of those who'd changed him. The doctor with ebony skin and a friendly smile.

A liar.

The helicopter landed in the distance. Every day, sometimes twice a day, it arrived, disgorging new passengers, carrying away others. Guarded by the men in black who carried guns.

He remembered guns.

Bad things.

Stay away.

Far, far away.

He knew this, and yet couldn't help but be drawn to the place that created him. A dangerous place to be if he was caught.

About to leave the edge of the forest, he paused.

Blinked as he saw the passenger on the helicopter disembark.

Smiled wide as he saw the doctor hugging a dark-skinned woman. Then kept his arm around her.

And a few days later, when that woman—younger than expected, with the most riveting blue eyes—went for a jog, Marcus kidnapped her for revenge.

FIND OUT WHAT HAPPENS NEXT IN *THE LIONMAN KIDNAPPING*

FOR MORE BOOKS BY EVE LANGLAIS OR TO RECEIVE HER NEWSLETTER, please visit EveLanglais.com